HUMAN FOR HIRE (4)
FRONTIER JUSTICE

COLLATERAL DAMAGE INCLUDED

T.R. HARRIS

TOM HARRIS CREATION, LLC

Copyright 2023
by Tom Harris Creations, LLC

Edited by
Lionel Dyck
Sherry Dixon
Grammarly
And of course…
Nikko, the Grammar Dog

This is a work of fiction. Names, characters, places, brands, media and incidents are either the product of the author's imagination or are used fictitiously. All rights reserved, without limiting the rights under copyright reserved above, no part of this publication may be reproduced, stored in or introduced into a retrieval system, or transmitted, in any form, or by any means (electronic, mechanically, photocopying, recording, or otherwise) without the prior written permission of both the copyright owner and the above publisher of this book.

HUMAN FOR HIRE (4)
FRONTIER JUSTICE

IN A ROUGH AND TUMBLE GALAXY...

Ruled by gun and muscle...

When you need the very best mercenary, bounty hunter, bodyguard or just straight muscle, you find a ...

Human for Hire

PROLOGUE

Driven by winds approaching two hundred miles per hour, a storm of crystallized carbon pellets buffeted Suma's faceplate, pitting the surface and penetrating deep enough to flake off a tiny portion of the polarizing film. A beam of light angled in, scorching his cheek along a line three inches long and eliciting an agonized moan from his lips. He turned his head quickly away from the blazing star.

"What is the issue?" Juhana asked, hearing the groan through his helmet's comm.

"A light breach," Suma replied. "Nothing serious, but I will have to keep my face turned away from Minos."

The pair of miners had just exited the nearest service access and were now forcing their way across the baked landscape toward the Number 3 Collector. Between them, they carried a replacement power module, protected from the elements by a shield of chromium, cobalt and nickel alloy infused with a polymer resin. The material was the same as their suits and would protect the unit from the harshest conditions the planet Sandicor could throw at it—at least under normal circumstances. But the coming flare season was promising to be a record breaker, with more frequent and powerful coronal mass ejections than ever before. This season would be one of the best, providing the colony with much-needed revenue and resources.

Then Suma cringed. It would also attract the worst elements in the galaxy. The flares could not be hidden; Chanco and his raiders would see them and know the harvest would be rich. They will come for their share.

But that was a concern for another day. The immediate issue was the worsening storm conditions exacerbated by the pre-flare eruptions Minos was giving off as a prelude to the major discharge. The star-facing side of Sandicor had been heated to nearly a thousand degrees, creating a more divergent climate between the light and dark sides of the planet. This increased the winds and turned the sand-like regolith that swirled within them into a corrosive soup that would rapidly eat through anything but the toughest material. Although their suits were made from an alloy five times stronger than steel, in an hour's time, the outer skin would be sanded away to nothing, meaning death for anyone remaining outside for long.

And that wasn't counting the radiation.

As Suma and Juhana neared the collector assembly, they found a modicum of relief from the shade it provided. The structure was massive and built to withstand even the most intense flares and the strongest winds. However, it, too, was made of the three-phase alloy, only fifty times thicker than the suits, and every eight years, the grid had to be replaced. It was an expensive and dangerous job, but something that had to be endured since the colony's very survival depended on the material harvested from the collectors.

The miners moved awkwardly toward the base of the assembly, fighting the prevailing wind direction. The flat surfaces of the carrying case acted like a sail, adding to the time it took to reach the collector. Both Suma and Juhana had made numerous power unit changeouts before, but never this close to a major eruption or in these conditions. The alarm had sounded only an hour earlier, signaling the fault and setting the colony into frantic motion. The collector would remain inoperative until the defective power module could be replaced, and without this collector, the harvest would be down by a third. That was unacceptable.

The collector array was a towering structure

shaped like a gigantic sail, anchored to the scorched surface by two-foot-thick cables and facing upward toward the fiery star. The facing grid was a technological marvel; it had to be considering the elusive material it was designed to gather. At its base was a squat equipment room, partially shielded from the angled starlight by a blackened rock a billion years old. If the stone had a consciousness, it would never have imagined the role it would play in the survival of the three hundred hardy souls that called Sandicor home. The collector was strategically placed at this location because of the rock. Unlike the collector grid, which operated in the full fury of the star Minos, the filters and power modules required additional protection against the elements. The outcropping helped shield the equipment from at least some of the intense heat and radiation.

The fact that the power unit had failed unexpectedly on Collector #3 meant that a fair portion of the harvest revenue would have to be spent on a new backup unit. Replacement parts were crucial to the operation of the colony since all three collectors were required to produce the bare minimum harvest; anything less would spell disaster.

The miners set the heavy box on the ground and pulled open the equipment shelter door. Fortunately, the rock partially protected them from the full force of the wind and the intensity of the starlight. But time was running short. Not only were they limited as to how long they could spend outside, but the major eruption could happen at any time. If they were still outside when that happened, no amount of three-phase alloy would save them.

Suma ducked inside the room and quickly unhooked the lines to the faulty power unit, then he and Juhana dragged the corrupted module out of the building and tossed it away. The wind caught the face of the unit, and it began tumbling, stopping about twenty feet away when it collided with another jagged rock.

Together, the miners lifted the replacement unit and moved it inside the shelter. After removing the module from the carrier, the hook-up was straightforward, and within ten minutes, the new unit was installed.

"Run a test," Suma ordered through the comm.

Others in the control room heard his command and activated the circuit.

"Full power—success!" said an excited female voice. Her name was Diyanna, and she was Juhana's promised. The concern for her mate-to-be was evident in her tone. "Number three is coming back online. Now hurry! You are well within the red zone for the coronal ejection. It could happen at any time."

"Understood," Suma said, even as he and Juhana were already on the move. The access hatch was only seventy feet from the collector, but in the tempest, it seemed like seventy miles. The pair leaned into the wind, with Suma now covering the pit in his helmet lens with a gloved hand, shading his face. They were staring directly into the full fury of the star, which sat only twenty-one million miles away from the tidally locked planet of Sandicor. On the star's surface, Suma could see the swirling yellows and orange of fusing hydrogen and helium, along with a fair number of darker patches where the cooler gases resided. It would be from here that the flare would erupt.

Although the colony prospered from the predictable cycle of flare eruptions, they could only estimate when the next major event would occur. Granted, their estimates were fairly accurate, usually within an hour or two. But still, they were estimates.

Suma led the pair toward the access shack, given priority over Juhana because of the hole in his polarizing film. They were still forty feet away when Diyanna's voice cried out in his comm.

"Eruption! Incoming flare!"

Suma glanced up at the star. He couldn't see the flare, not yet; the light and radiation would take just under two minutes to reach the planet. But the operators in the control room knew the truth.

"Hurry, Juhana!" Suma cried.

"I am doing my best, my friend. Do not wait for me. If you must, get to the hatch and close it."

"I would never do that ... and leave you outside."

"You may have to. We both know the truth."

And the truth was that the miners could only move so fast in their suits, and adding the impeding force of the wind, it would be a miracle if either of them made it to the hatch in time.

"Give me a count!" Suma ordered.

"Seventy-four seconds," said Diyanna's trembling voice.

Suma reached the access hatch with twenty-nine seconds to spare. He swung open the door and stepped inside, knowing that simply being inside the enclosure would not save him against the flare. The door would have to be closed.

"Juhana, hurry!"

The silver-clad figure of his friend was still twenty feet away and struggling against the wind.

"Fifteen seconds! Hurry, Juhana," Diyanna cried.

And then Juhana stopped and raised one of his six hands.

"Goodbye, Diyanna; I will not make it. I will not even try. Suma, my friend, do what you must."

"No, I cannot!"

"Five seconds. Four, three…"

And then Suma closed the hatch.

The power of a flare striking the planet was deceptive and came in stages. At first, an onslaught of deadly radiation and electromagnetic energy struck Sandicor, traveling at the speed of light and reaching the planet in only a couple of minutes after the eruption. The colony was protected against such a strike, but not anyone on the surface. The coronal mass ejection itself would only last a few seconds on the surface of the star, but the ejecta—the stream of charged particles and minute amounts of more exotic material—would take roughly seventy-eight hours to reach Sandicor. This ejecta was what the collectors gathered and then filtered, including the elusive Element 129. Until the last remnants of the flare faded, no one would be allowed onto the surface. By then, there wouldn't be much of Juhana's body to recover.

Suma leaned against the rock wall of the access tunnel, remorse and pain flooding his senses. He and Juhana were born on Sandicor during the same year, and although they were of different species, they were more like brothers than mere friends. With so few children born on the planet, they played together and shared their dreams while learning how to tend to the harvest from their fathers and mothers. Once reaching worker age, they spent the past nine standard years tending to the collectors and helping refine the crop. And now, they had nearly died together. Suma knew Juhana was right; he would have died with his friend, making a last-ditch effort to pull him inside. That was why Juhana stopped advancing. He did not want to leave Suma the option.

Just then, the names of Kanis and Dalicon came to Suma's mind, two other miners who had recently lost their lives while mining E-129. And they were just the latest on a long list of miners who had given their all for the good of the colony. A miner's life on Sandicor was not an easy one, nor was it safe. But all the inhabitants of the colony were born here, and although only a few restless souls ever left Sandicor for a better life elsewhere, the others remained. This was their home, no matter how hellish it may be. Even so, Suma would grieve the loss of his friend—his best friend. It was what the miners of Sandicor did, and far too often.

Four days later, Juhana's body was recovered. Diyanna insisted on viewing the remains, but she quickly regretted the decision. The suit had been compromised, but that came long after the intense radiation had fried the body. It was a grisly scene and one the young female would never forget.

Miners on Sandicor died for many reasons but seldom was it from exposure to a flare. After three hundred years, they were too versed in the precautions to let that happen. But on occasion, it did. Juhana's charred body was a vivid reminder of the reality they all faced.

Eight days after the flare, the members of the

colony gathered in the Grand Hall or watched on broadcasts as the yield was announced. Suma was present in the Hall, seated to the left of Elder Tansin, the current leader of the colony.

Tansin was a grizzled, yellow-skinned creature of a species whose name Suma couldn't remember if he'd ever been told. The colony was made up of eighteen unique species of Prime, each having come to the planet in the early days to work the harvest. By now, no one paid attention to race except when it came to mating. Other than that, everyone was simply a member, a compatriot sharing in the dangers and rewards of a life on Sandicor.

Tansin stood at the podium.

"Giving grace for the efforts of our friends Suma and Juhana, we have had a very successful first harvest of the season," he announced solemnly. "And in honor of his selfless act of courage and sacrifice, a memorial plaque will be affixed to the Grand Hall in honor of Juhana Semion. Let us never forget the service our two friends gave for the good of the colony." The Elder looked at Suma and nodded.

Suma fought back the tears. He didn't feel he deserved to be honored; he had closed the door, leaving his friend outside to die. It would have been more of an honor to have joined him in death rather than selfishly save his own life. Unfortunately, that was not how the others saw it, including Diyanna. She avowed her respect for Suma, holding no grudge for what he had done. Her actions only made Suma feel worse.

But now Tansin was continuing. "The most recent flare brought forth with it a particularly rich crop of E-129, in fact, the most we have ever recovered in a single event. Without Number 3 in operation, the yield would not have been anywhere near what it was. As a result, we have gathered *ninety-eight* full units."

A few of the people in the Hall knew the number, but most did not. Now they gasped before a few began clapping. Soon, the Hall was filled with celebratory cheering. Even Suma forgot his self-pity and joined in the festive mood.

Ninety-eight units were the equivalent of three or four major flares. And this had come in only one. And with the current demand for E-129, that would mean prosperity for the colony, a chance to build some reserves for the hard times that were bound to come.

Watching and listening to his friends and colony mates rejoice in the good news made Suma temper his guilt. This was indeed good news. He would let himself honor Juhana by sharing in the joy the harvest brought to others. It was appropriate.

"And now, please, please," Tansin was saying, trying to regain control of the room. Slowly, the crowd was quieting down. And that was when the smile left the Elder's face, for there was another message coming through the speakers and circulating throughout the colony.

"Attention! Attention! Two spacecraft have landed at Access Port Nine. I repeat, two spacecraft have landed."

The voice was strained and provided no further explanation with the announcement. None was needed.

Chanco Kantos was on Sandicor.

With his newfound status within the colony, Suma was invited to meet with the raiders. Within minutes, Chanco's troops were moving unrestricted throughout the maze of underground tunnels and caverns. They entered abodes and rummaged through personal belongings, looking for anything of value they had not found on their previous visits to Sandicor. But as intrusive and insulting as the thefts may have been, that was only the beginning.

Chanco Kantos was a stocky creature with reddish skin. He was central Prime, with two legs, two arms and an oblong head with inset eyes, an expressive mouth and a fairly large nose. His ears were pointed, and a pair of knobby, one-inch-long horns poked from his forehead. He strode into the governing chambers without invitation, accompanied by his support entourage of Laznor, Bensin and Vor. His lieutenants were each of different races, as were most of his forty-plus raiders that filtered through the colony. Within the meeting room, the four aliens plopped down in chairs, with Bensin draping a long leg over an armrest. None appeared intimidated in the least. They knew the colony was no threat to them. That point had been demonstrated in blood beginning four years ago when Chanco first came to Sandicor. Since then, the resistance has been more subdued, almost to the point of nonexistent. What was the point? The raiders were killers, and the miners were not.

"So, my good friend Tansin, I saw from the reports that you recently encountered a record flare from your Lifegiver, Minos." Chanco's voice was deep and accented, with certain letters and syllables spoken with a trill in his tongue. This caused confusion with the translation bug, with Suma having a terrible time understanding the alien. Still, he hung on to every word; misunderstandings in the past had resulted in the death of colony members simply from the frustration Chanco felt from having to repeat himself. "You must tell me the good news. As colony members ourselves, we wish to share in the bounty. Please, tell us, Tansin. What was the yield?"

"You are not members…." Suma was shocked to have heard the words come from his mouth, even as they were issued forth as a whisper. His heart leaped into his throat, and his eyes grew wide as Chanco shifted his attention to the young miner.

"You are called Suma, are you not?" the raider said to him, the first time Chanco had ever spoken to him directly. "A young spirit coming of age within the colony."

"Yes, he is Suma," Tansin said quickly. "He is a valuable member of the colony."

Chanco studied Suma for a moment, a thin grin on his lips. "You do not approve of my presence here, young Suma? Why is that?"

Suma was taken aback by the question. *Because you are a killer and thief who has come to rob us of our essential bounty, that is why!* That was what he wanted to say. But instead, he remained silent.

"Please speak freely, miner," Chanco pleaded. "I am curious to learn of the colony's impression of my people and me. It has been nearly a standard year since we were last here. What attitudes have changed since our last visit?"

Suma looked to Tansin, who gazed back at him with sad eyes. The situation was out of his hands. Suma's fate was now in the hands of the raider.

"Forgive me," Suma managed to say at last. "I lost a good friend in the last harvest. His death still weighs heavy on my soul."

"That is understandable," Chanco said with sincerity. "I hope his death was not in vain."

Suma felt as if he'd been slapped in the face. The raider's presence on Sandicor did make Juhana's death meaningless, but dare he express his true feelings? At that moment, Suma's past guilt resurfaced. He should have died on the surface of the planet, along with Juhana. Now, he felt it only fair that he should die defending his friend and colony. Someone had to speak the truth.

"Yes, his death was in vain … with you here to take our harvest, the harvest Juhana gave his life to create. He did it not for your benefit but for the good of the people of Sandicor, for the colony. When you leave after having raided our belongings and wealth, his death will be meaningless. He should have survived, and you should leave here with far less than you will. I could have died with him. Now, I am willing to give my life to let the truth be known about you and your raiders. You are not welcome here; you have never been welcome. All you do is take and provide nothing for the community. You are parasites, beasts that haunt our nightmares. Do what you will with me. I care not, not if I must witness further decay of my colony from the likes of you."

The smile never left Chanco's mouth as he listened patiently to Suma's last testament. Now all he had to do was to draw his weapon and place a bolt into his chest. Suma was prepared for that. In fact, he'd never felt stronger, more sure of anything he'd ever done in his life. He had spit in the face of the demon. The demon be damned!

And then Chanco moved his hands, but not to grasp his weapon, but to begin a slow clap. After a moment, he stopped and looked at Tansin, who was pale and trembling from fear. There was no telling what revenge the raider would take on the colony for Suma's insolence.

"This is indeed the spirit of the young I was speaking of. It brings vitality to the community and keeps the will to live thriving from generation to generation. Without it, your colony could wither and die, which would do me no good." He looked back to Suma. "Relax, young miner; I will not kill you today. I welcome the clearing of the tension between us, and I respect your honesty and courage—"

"Then you will leave and take no harvest? Let us survive!"

Chanco batted his eyes several times, stunned by the interruption. "What is this, Laznor," he said, addressing his second in command. "I express a moment of gratitude, of leniency, and this is the reward I get? More demands ... on me!" His eyes never left Suma. "No, I will not leave without my share of the harvest."

"It is not *your* harvest!"

And now the weapon appeared in Chanco's hand. He leaned forward in his chair and pointed the barrel at Suma's forehead. "Do you wish to die, young Suma? Is that why you provoke me as you do? I gave you a chance to express your feelings; you did. Now, be quiet. You are no longer a participant in these affairs but merely an observer. Tansin!"

"Yes, Lord Chanco."

"What was the harvest yield? And do not lie to me; I will verify before I leave."

"Ninety-four units."

The raider recoiled, his eyes still locked on Suma and his weapon aimed at his forehead.

"Ninety-four! That is truly impressive. I see now why you would fight so hard to keep it." He lowered the gun, and Suma breathed again. "You do realize what a significant amount that is. With the proliferation of energy credits backed by the products that produce said energy, E-129 is becoming one of the rarest elements in the galaxy. Even the large energy firms, such as Maris-Kliss and Raynor, are falling short in their breeder reactors. Raw E-129, in its purest form, is demanding a premium. And from what the scientists say, Minos is moving into a period of more frequent flares, meaning an even richer harvest to come. Because of that, I will only take sixty units. You must know how generous that is of me. Thirty-eight units will be enough to restock your colony and help with future harvests throughout the season."

Chanco then turned to Tansin, and his eyes grew

hard. "But be assured, I will not be as generous with future harvests. I will make up for my loss with a higher percentage in the future. We need the E-129 as much as you do, maybe more. You have the means of creating wealth; we do not. All we get is what we take from others. And in the wake of the Klin invasion, my people are hurting because *others* are hurting. Tansin, you should consider yourselves fortunate. Your colony is one of the few prosperous entities in this part of the galaxy. I will not starve you to death, but I will leave you with the incentive to make each harvest the best it can be."

"The harvest is what it will be. Only Minos controls that, not us," Tansin waxed philosophically.

"That may be true, but make the effort anyway. If I find my time coming here is no longer profitable, I may take it all and let your pitiful colony die. After all, who would want to live on such a slime pit as Sandicor? I would be doing you all a favor if I was to end your miserable existence. Now, get us our share, and we will be on our way. But we will return. It is estimated another flare should erupt in forty standard days." He looked back at Suma. "Hopefully, by then, all this animosity will have faded because next time, I will not be so gracious. Confront me again as you did this time, Suma, and you will surely die. Is that understood?"

Suma nodded, not emphatically, but enough. He was surprised he was still alive but also guilty for being so. As with Juhana's death, he'd been robbed again of the opportunity to die for a cause. Perhaps next time....

"That was foolish and uncalled for!" Tansin barked at Suma after the raiders left. "*You* may not fear death, but he could have easily taken his vengeance out on others just to spite you. What were you thinking?"

"I was thinking what everyone else is thinking; only I voiced my concerns."

"And nearly got yourself killed."

"I did what I thought was right."

Tansin's office was rapidly filling with people from the colony, around twenty-five so far, who had come to the governing chambers to protest this latest affront to the colony. Not only had sixty units of E-129 been taken, but also hundreds of other items, including personal mementos, jewelry and more. After all the raids over the past four years, there wasn't much more to take, and the citizens were at their wit's end.

"What are we to do?" an elderly female asked Tansin. "We cannot go on like this. They took a datapad with videos of my family. I cannot get those memories back."

The Elder was then inundated with a deluge of similar stories and feelings.

"Please, calm yourselves," Tansin said. "I, too, feel your pain and suffering."

"Then what are you to do about it?" asked a burly, yellow-skinned miner named Rilos. He had an angry scar across his forehead, the result of a cave-in in the lower tunnels from five years ago. He was one of the lucky ones. "We cannot continue letting Chanco come as he pleases."

"But we have no way to stop him," said a voice in the crowd.

"And if we resist, it will only lead to more death, more hardship."

Suma had had enough. Twice he had cheated death, and whether he wanted to admit it or not, he was feeling rather invincible.

"We must do something!" he yelled above the din of the crowd. He caught Tansin's scowl of disapproval, but he was already committed. "We must fight back."

"But how?" someone asked. "We are not fighters—"

"And we have no weapons," said another.

"Then we will have to learn to fight," Suma addressed the first speaker. "And we will buy weapons," he said to the other.

"And you will get yourselves killed," Tansin said. "You could get us *all* killed."

"We are dying already," Suma countered. "Only slowly and at the whim of Chanco and his raiders. He said it himself; if he cannot take enough from us, he will take everything and let us die. Either we fight back, or we slowly wither as a plant does when the light goes out, or the water stops flowing." He turned to the crowd. "And you all know this will continue unless we stand up for ourselves. The only thing creatures like Chanco understands is strength, and until now, we have been weak, compliant … victims. We are many, and they are few. If we had enough weapons, we could put an end to this tyranny. We could make the colony flourish again, as we once did. What would the sixty units of 129 mean to us if we still had it and with more to come? What if we could keep it all? How good could life be on Sandicor if only Chanco didn't exist? It is time for us to make a stand."

"What do you propose, Suma?" the miner Rilos asked. Suma could see the fire in his eyes.

"When we go to Nefar to sell the harvest, we should take some of those credits and buy weapons."

"It will not leave much for the colony," said a female in protest.

"It is a sacrifice we must make," Suma replied. "If we can stop Chanco, then all future harvests will be ours to keep—all of it. It is the only way to save the colony."

"Or kill it," Tansin stated.

"We are dying already," said a voice in the crowd, which brought a chorus of agreement from others.

The discussion continued for half an hour before a decision was made. Suma would lead a delegation to the planet Nefar, where they would seek to purchase weapons to arm the colony. If Chanco finds that the cost of stealing from the colony is too high, then he will leave them alone. That was the final word. After that, preparations began for the journey. And they had a deadline. Chanco would return after the next flare event. They had to be ready by then.

Suma was consumed by his anger and his guilt, which easily canceled the doubt he had in his mind. There would be deaths; that was a given. Perhaps Suma would be among them. He did not care; in fact, he was counting on it.

1

"That bastard, Tidus!" Adam Cain exclaimed under his breath. "He's trying to get me killed."

There was no other explanation.

Adam could vividly recall the words of his Starfire Security boss, the Juirean Tidus Fe Nolan, as he described his current assignment.

"I have a juicy bounty hunt for you, something that might fit your current mood: A gangster with an army surrounding him. It should give you ample opportunity to smash some alien skulls and vent some of that frustration you're feeling."

Well, that would have been fine if it wasn't for the fact that Tidus was being literal this time.

Adam lay on his stomach, hidden in the yellow brush of a small rise about a mile out from the fugitive's compound, electronic binoculars pressed against his eyes. He wore a ghillie suit infused with the grass of the field on his back to provide better camouflage. He'd just finished his first on-site survey of the scene and was reassessing the reality of the mission. He couldn't believe what he was seeing.

First of all, Tidus wasn't exaggerating—not this time. The fugitive *did* have an army protecting him; a real army made up of professional soldiers with uniforms, combat-grade weapons, and whose movements and temperament spoke of excellent training. As would be expected.

Their boss—some beast name Zankor—was a one-time general—or whatever they called military commanders on the planet Nefar—who had attempted to overthrow the planetary government a few months back. Now, the Nefareans were offering a three-million-energy-credit reward for his capture and return to the planet.

The money aside, this meant that Adam was not only going after an experienced and high-ranking military officer but someone who brought thirty-five hundred of his most loyal troops with him when he fled the planet. And now this not-so-insignificant force was hiding out on a planet in a nearby system as they planned their next move.

Adam rolled over in the grass and looked up at the blue sky above. It was a beautiful day on … hell; he forgot the name of the planet he was on. Oh, well, it didn't matter. It was nice here, and Adam just wanted to take a few moments to relax before setting his mind on the details of the mission. He'd had a hell of a crappy past six months and was looking to regroup. But that wasn't going to happen if he had to fight his way through thirty-five hundred loyal fighters to reach his fugitive. And the soldiers weren't there for the money, not like an army of mercenaries. These guys had to be full-blown fanatics.

And besides that … everyone had horns.

That annoying fact made Adam cringe when he scanned the troops in the settlement below. He'd seen a lot of species with horns before, and they'd always proved to be the most problematic for him. But these guys might top the list. Their species resembled upright-walking bulls, with incredibly broad and muscular shoulders, bulging legs and a head made like, well, a bull. And then the horns. These weren't tiny token horns like most others he'd seen. No, these were Texas Longhorn types. Not only that, but they appeared to sharpen the ends and attach silver caps to the tips to give them even more durability in battle. It seemed to be a matter of pride for these bastards.

Adam looked up at the soothing sky and scowled. "Fuck it; I'm not going to relax until I figure this out."

He rolled back onto his stomach and brought the binoculars up to his eyes.

It was obvious this would have to be a snatch-and-run. There was no way even someone like *The Human* could single-handily fight his way through the army to reach the general and then get away safely. And Adam had no backup. He was on his own.

It would have to be a covert op. Somehow, he would have to slip in unseen, grab the bull-of-a-general by the horns, so to speak, and then spirit him away before anyone found out.

Three million credits for the job. Hell, it would take ten times that much to adequately—

Adam smelled the soldier only a split second before the big beast plowed his deadly horns into the ground directly in front of him, throwing black dirt into his face, nose and mouth. If it hadn't been for the binoculars pressed against his eyes, Adam would have been blinded when the creature charged. As it was, he was able to roll sideways just in time to avoid the silver tip of the Nefarean's left horn.

But then the beast spun around and scooped Adam up onto his block head. Fortunately, the smallish Human fit *between* the horns of the nine-foot-tall creature and not skewered on them, a fact that upset the Nefarean bull to no end. Adam wrapped his arms around the thick skull, doing everything he could to hold tight as the beast threw his head from side to side, trying to dislodge the Human so he could take another stab at him with his horns.

But the horns weren't the only weapons the alien

had. He also had two beefy arms and hands, which he used to tug on Adam's legs, trying to pull him from his head. It was all Adam could do to hold on.

Adam's face was pressed against the boney forehead, only inches from one of the bulbous black eyes. It was as big as a billiard ball and shiny like the eight ball. It kept rolling from side to side, revealing a thin line of white along the edges that made the orb look manic. The darn thing also stuck out about two inches from the eye socket ... which gave Adam an idea.

The eye locked on the Human as he stared at the orb, wondering if he had the balls to do it. But then Adam smiled a full tooth grin that—in this case—*was* a death challenge.

"Don't worry, buddy," Adam said to the alien. "I'm not going to like this, either."

Then Adam leaned over and bit down on the bulging orb with all his might. And if that wasn't disgusting enough, the eyeball burst, sending a rush of putrid-tasting retinal fluid shooting into the back of his throat and down into his stomach.

As much as Adam hated what he'd just done, the Nefarean bull hated it even more. He yelped out in pain, dropping to his knees and scraping his head with his long arms fighting a losing battle against the pain. Adam let go of the head and slipped off, careful as he passed between the deadly horns. The beast writhed in pain, completely forgetting about the Human, his high-pitched yelping becoming more pronounced by the second.

Once Adam was clear of the injured soldier, he pulled his MK-88 hybrid bolt launcher from its holster. The weapon had a ballistic capability, but that would be too loud. Instead, Adam chose the flash option as he stepped up to the screaming creature, pressed the barrel against his exposed chest, and triggered the weapon. The flash of the plasma bolt was covered by the proximity of the weapon to the alien's skin. The bolt entered the body, and a split second later, the mighty beast lay dead.

Adam didn't kill the alien to put him out of his misery; he did it to shut the damn thing up. His screaming might attract even more bulls.

Now Adam vomited. He'd wanted to ever since he bit down on the alien's eye. In hindsight, Adam would never react to the word *bullseye* the same way ever again.

The momentum of the short battle had carried the combatants over the crest of the hill to the opposite side from the encampment, but that wouldn't mean anything if the alien had already called in the intruder's presence to his command. Adam searched the body for a comm device. He had one, which was expected. The alien was a trained soldier, and even if he didn't make a report prior to attacking Adam, he would eventually have to check-in.

Adam returned to the hilltop and found his binoculars. A quick scan of the camp below showed no unusual activity. That was a relief, but not much.

And then the comm device sounded.

Adam ran back to the body and took the communicator out of its holder. The Nefareans had once been part of the Juirean Expansion before the Klin invasion, so their language was part of the Universal Translation Database. Adam was able to understand the message.

"Pep-One Dallon, report. Confirm sighting. Pep-One, report."

Adam listened to the timbre of the voice before activating the communicator, attempting to imitate the sound. "Pep-One reporting. False report. Nothing here."

There was a delay on the comm before the soldier spoke again. "Understood, Pep-One. Maintain position. Thirty minutes to shift change. Confirm blue. Acknowledge."

"Acknowledged, confirm blue," Adam said before breaking the link.

Then he grimaced. There was something odd about the exchange. It sounded like a coded ID check.

Adam activated the comm again, this time not using his fake Nefarean accent. "Pep-One here," he said.

"Go ahead, Pep-One," said a skeptical voice.

"I didn't fool you for a second, did I?" Adam asked with a laugh in his voice.

"No, you did not."

"Hey, it was worth a try."

"Remain where you are and do not resist. We are coming to retrieve you."

"I'm afraid I can't do that."

"Then you will be killed."

"Maybe, but first, you'll have to catch me."

Adam clicked off the link again and scrambled for the ridge. There was a lot more activity in the camp now, as motorized vehicles were being loaded with soldiers and heading for the exits. It looked as if half the camp was mobilizing to look for him.

Good, let them come, Adam thought as he moved along the ridge before following a line of rocks jutting out of the ground. If the Nefareans want to find him, they would have to look in the last place they would expect him to be ... *their encampment.*

2

There was a line of reddish rocks jutting out of the hillside, providing cover as Adam moved toward the base of the hill. It would get him to the north end of the encampment, where he could use the various tents and supply trucks to get inside. He'd already narrowed down the structures to a handful where the general might be staying. They were the largest and most opulent. Security around them wasn't any more elaborate than elsewhere in the camp since only Nefarean bulls occupied the base. It wouldn't be too hard to make entry into the tents to find the general.

The question Adam had was ... *what then?*

The Human didn't fear any alien; that confidence was grounded in thirty-plus years of fighting the smelly bastards from one end of the galaxy to the other. But the Nefareans were something else altogether. The average alien was around seven feet tall, which at nine feet, made the bulls the exception rather than the rule. And they were strong—for aliens. Again, Adam didn't fear a stronger alien. All that meant is they gave something up for the added strength, and mainly speed and coordination. His brief battle with the sentry didn't tell him much, except that the Nefareans placed too much emphasis on their horns. The guard was armed with a bolt launcher; he could have easily shot Adam. Instead, he chose to play games with him using his impressive horns. And that cost him his life.

A line of vehicles moved out of the encampment and up the hill toward Adam's last known position. At the opposite base of the hill was Adam's rented transport. They would find it there and reason he was on foot, heading into the hilly region to the north and headed for the city of Issennor. It was the largest settlement for hundreds of miles and where Adam had the *Arieel* parked. But even if the Nefareans thought he was on foot, there was no telling how long they would keep up the pursuit without a trail to follow. They would find the body of the guard, and that might give them more incentive to continue the search. But eventually, they would return to the camp. Adam had to be long gone—with the general—by then.

Adam scooted along the back perimeter of a large

tent before sprinting between massive half-track vehicles, making his way closer to the first target structure. There were plenty of bulls still wandering the camp, but they were concentrated at the other end near what looked to be barracks and supply tents. The command tents were placed off to themselves. Still, Adam had no idea what he would do if and when he found Zankor —if he did before being spotted.

Being much smaller than a Nefarean was an advantage for the Human. At one point, he had to dive under a transport as two bulls suddenly appeared, turning toward him when they did. The clearance under the vehicle was spacious, and Adam held his breath as the creatures walked by. This was when Adam noticed they didn't wear shoes. Instead, they had hooved feet that could undoubtedly be used as weapons if need be. The damn animals were built for battle. Adam had been lucky to take out one of them. In a standup fight, things might have ended differently.

After a few minutes, Adam moved on, coming to a small landing field not too far from his target tents. A pair of quadcopters were there, not being used in the search. He moved over to one and looked inside the cockpit. Standard controls, nothing exotic and a spacious interior. This gave Adam an idea for exfiltration once he found the general.

Adam returned to the tents.

He still wore the ghillie suit, which was a lightweight mesh of bands where he laced native grass to cover his back. Now the jacket was too cumbersome to move within a structure. He slipped out of the suit and stashed it behind a stack of supply crates before moving up to the side of the first tent.

Adam took out a black-bladed K-BAR knife and cut a small slit in the canvas material. Peeking inside, he saw a smallish enclosure within the larger structure with a massive bed and strange harness hanging from a supporting trellis. There were two loops on the end of the harness. *For the horns?* Adam questioned. Otherwise, how would they keep from tearing the bed—and their bedmates—apart as they slept? He shrugged. The aliens had evolved with the horns; he was sure they had it worked out.

And speaking of the horns, from what Adam witnessed during his survey, the sexes could be determined by the presence or absence of the horns. Obviously, the females didn't have them, matching how Earth-born bovines had evolved. And they were smaller than the males. Still, Adam wasn't looking forward to tangling with even a female Nefarean.

Adam enlarged the cut he'd made in the tent wall so he could enter the sleeping quarters. Although the bed was large, he figured all Nefarean beds were big to accommodate the nine-foot-tall aliens. So, this didn't mean the general slept here. But he had to take a look.

He crouched down and moved to the exit flap to

the room, and looked into the larger part of the tent. There were six bulls in the central room, four at a table and two seated at desks. Their heads were tilted down slightly, concentrating on their work. There were other flaps along the perimeter of the room, but nothing spoke to Adam, saying this was the general's tent. It looked more like support staff.

He moved outside again and slipped over to the next tent, a mirror of the first one. After making a cut in the fabric, he saw the interior of this tent was laid out differently. The sleeping quarters were bigger, and there was an open wardrobe with grey uniforms on hangers. Epaulets with gold and blue shoulder boards were clipped to the clothing, something a high-ranking officer might wear. Adam didn't have a picture of the general, but he had observed the differing ranks as he surveyed the encampment. The occupant of this bedroom was pretty far up the chain of command.

The Human slipped inside the room and moved to the door flap. This tent was cut into more rooms, and as far as he could tell, they were vacant. The Nefareans gave off a particularly strong odor; in fact, they smelled like a stockyard. It was the trait that saved Adam's life on the hilltop. But now he couldn't rely on that sense to help much. The whole camp smelled awful, but the interior of the tent wasn't quite so bad, making him believe no one was home.

Perhaps the general was with the troops hunting

him. That would be bad. But why would he? A single observer wasn't worth the effort. Sure, he'd killed a soldier, but that was what soldiers were for. But still, Adam couldn't be sure Zankor was even in the camp. However, this did appear to be his living quarters. Adam would wait here until he returned. It would also give him time to figure out what to do if he did.

Adam was in the bedroom, studying the double harness above the bed, trying to imagine how the horns would fit in it. He hoped it was horns; otherwise, the Nefareans were a lot kinkier than he thought. Just then, he heard voices outside. He crouched down and pulled the door flap back as a pair of bulls came into the outer room.

"Continue the search into the night; make it into a training exercise. The troops have grown lethargic and bored. This will help with their mood, especially if they catch the spy." The words were spoken by a Nefarean male with greying temples and horns, yellower than most of the others. An old bull? He was wearing grey pants and a matching shirt with no rank insignia. Only the top dog could get away with that.

"I agree," said the second bull. "But perhaps we should also alert our spies in Issennor. Have them watch the spaceport for any suspicious activity."

Zankor waved a hand at his subordinate. "As you wish, Zoris. Another chance for training. We have all grown complacent as we have hidden out on this rock, but that will not last forever. We must be ready for when we are called home."

"Yes, Warden. I will tend to the training operation myself."

"You do that. For the time being, I will be in my quarters until the time of the communication with Nefar. There have been changes afoot. I hope for good news with this next link."

"As do we all." The second officer left the tent.

As Adam watched, he sensed that the general—or warden—was alone, with no one in any of the adjoining rooms. The big bull stretched his long arms, gripping his horns with his hands and then twisting his back. Adam heard the crack from where he was hiding. And then Zankor farted.

Damn! It didn't take long for the putrid gas to filter throughout the tent, making Adam's eyes water. And here, Adam thought *Humans* were foul creatures.

And then Zankor made a move toward the bedroom.

Adam slipped back from the doorway, hiding behind the curtain and the cover flaps for the wardrobe. The warden/general entered the room and moved to the bed, where he began to unbutton his shirt, his back to Adam.

Now came the dilemma. How could Adam subdue the big beast without giving him time to raise the alarm? He could stun the officer with a lower setting on his MK, but would that even work on a creature this large? Adam had no choice but to try.

Dialing the MK to stun, Adam moved out of his hiding place and stepped behind the general. Without waiting for the targeting computer in the weapon to lock on, Adam pulled the trigger when he was only about a foot behind Zankor. The flash was hidden from the rest of the camp by the thick canvas walls of the tent. At least Adam hoped it was.

Zankor lurched forward, falling face-first onto the bed before he attempted to roll over, still conscious but affected by the low-intensity bolt. He swung his head from side to side, the metal-clad tips of his yellow horns tearing into the bedding. A muddled groan came from his mouth. It wasn't loud enough to be heard outside the tent, but it got louder the longer Adam let it go on.

Another stun bolt quieted Zankor down, but it took a third to knock him out completely. The beast lay on the bed, breathing heavily, the bulging eyes covered now with thick, grey eyelids.

Now what? Adam thought. Then he jumped on the bed and began unhooking the straps to the horn harness. He tied the bull's hands behind his back and then placed a thick strap in the general's mouth, tying it behind his head. And then Adam remembered about the hooved feet. A kick from one of those would be enough to put Adam down for the count, so he also tied the legs together with the straps.

Now, the Human had an unconscious, nine-foot-tall beast with a four-foot-wide span of deadly horns lying on the bed. Testing the weight, Adam was rewarded with another fact of alien life in the galaxy. Most of the taller ones were light as a feather, meaning they weren't as heavy as they appeared. In Adam's experience, it took lighter gravity to produce tall creatures, and lighter gravity meant weaker and thinner bones. Also, the musculature didn't have to be as robust as a being that evolved on a heavy gravity world, such as the Humans of Earth. Adam found he could lift the bull and carry him in his arms ... if Adam's arms were long enough. But they weren't, so he would have to settle for dragging the alien to the quadcopter.

Cutting an even larger slit in the tent wall, Adam took Zankor by his horns and dragged him through the opening. It was only about fifty yards to the small airfield, but it did involve Adam having to double the distance by dragging the sleeping bull along the side of tents and then stashing him behind the wheels of transports until the occasional soldier passed. The ground of the compound was covered in thick, yellow grass, which, although there were still drag tracks, weren't as prominent as they would have been if the surface was only dirt.

To Adam's amazement, he made it to the airfield without being spotted or an alarm rising from the command tent. He brought Zankor around to the passenger door of one of the copters and shoved him inside, taking the seatbelts and tying the big beast into the chair.

Then Adam rushed to the second quadcopter and pulled open the engine bay door. He began pulling out wires and other connections, doing all he could to cripple the airship. Not sure if he'd done enough, he moved to the cockpit when a clever idea came to him. There were dual controls, a pair of joysticks used to pilot the craft. Adam used his Human strength to snap both of them off at the point where they joined the control module. The bulls may have spare parts for just about anything else that could go wrong with the copter, but would they have extra joysticks? He hoped they wouldn't. It would be like going to an auto mechanic and asking for a new steering wheel. They could get one ordered, but the chances of them having one in stock would be slim.

Again, Adam hoped so.

He rushed back to the first copter and checked on his passenger. He was still out, but for how long was anyone's guess? Adam had to get into the air before he woke up. Once airborne, the beast may have second thoughts about causing a ruckus if it could mean them crashing.

As he'd observed before, the controls were standard, and Adam surveyed them before starting the engine. He wanted to be ready to go the moment the rotors were at speed. The vehicle was a four-bladed affair with the rotors enclosed in a set of white rings open on the top and bottom and able to change orientation to create lift and forward or backward motion. Adam had flown craft like these before. The only difference was the cockpit in this one was huge to accommodate the big aliens. Adam spent far too long searching for the controls to move the seat up so he could grasp the control stick. And then he pressed the start button.

Although the rotors were enclosed within their housings, they were still quite noisy as the speed increased. It would only take about five seconds to achieve take-off speed, but that was enough time for heads to turn toward the new sound. Adam sat in the glass bubble of the cockpit, in full sight of anyone looking his way. And look they did.

And then he began to lift off, slowly at first but gaining speed every second.

Bulls were now moving onto the landing field, looking up and wondering who had authorized the flight. Adam looked down, making eye contact with several of the soldiers. He could tell they knew he was an alien, but few grasped the reality that he was the alien that half the camp was out looking for. But then some sharp-eyed Nefarean spotted Zankor slumped over in the passenger seat. Even so, it took a few seconds for him to make the connection.

By then, Adam was a hundred feet in the air and moving quickly over the encampment. He kept his altitude low over the tents so he wouldn't make an easy target for the alien's Xan-fi rifles. Soon, the quadcopter was away from the camp and, with no air pursuit following.

Issennor was north of the encampment, but the ground between here and there was covered with a couple of thousand wild bulls just itching for something to shoot at. And on their armored vehicles were missiles and flash cannon. Therefore, Adam took a southern route away from the camp, over the desert. He'd swing back around once he had some distance between him and the camp and approach the city from the east. It would also throw off the ground troops expecting him to fly over their position.

The copter had a full battery charge, and with the second vehicle disabled, Adam was confident no air pursuit was coming. He relaxed. He'd be back in

Issennor in about an hour and in space thirty minutes after that.

All in all, this three-million-credit bounty had been one of his easiest to collect. That should make Tidus happy.

And then Zankor woke up.

3

Adam had no idea how long the general had been conscious, but it was obvious he didn't just snap out of the effects of the stun bolts fully awake and ready for action. He had to have been lying there, biding his time.

With his hands and feet tied, he still had his formidable horns to use as weapons. Zankor whipped his head in Adam's direction, bringing the left horn within an inch of the Human's cheek. It ripped into the padded back of the seat before he whipped it back and into the instrument panel.

"Are you crazy?" Adam yelled. "We're five hundred feet in the air. Do you want to die?"

Zankor's response was muffled by the strap in his mouth.

"Calm down!" Adam added, but the bull didn't

heed the warning. He continued to thrash about the cockpit, ripping apart the front panel and causing system alarms to scream.

Adam was reaching for his MK for another stun bolt when the front starboard rotor failed. The problem with quadcopters was they needed all four blades turning to maintain flight integrity. All Adam could do at this point was decrease the power to the other motors and try for the softest landing he could. But that wasn't going to happen.

The port side rotors lifted the craft up on that side, sending the copter slanting over to starboard, slicing through the air, and heading for the surface.

"You dumb bastard!" Adam yelled. "Now we're both going to die."

The craft rolled completely over, which gave Adam an idea. He reversed the blades in the port rotors, which were now facing down on the starboard side. The copter slowed before angling up on the right side and then slicing toward the surface from the other direction. In the end, Adam gained nothing except to slow the vehicle as it got closer to the ground. But at least the craft was oriented right … until it listed to starboard again. Adam repeated his last maneuver two more times as the copter neared the ground. The last time had them angled to starboard and still dropping at a decent—and deadly—speed.

The copter crashed and the canopy crumbled on

Zankor's side, breaking Adam's chair away from the supports and sending him falling into the Nefarean, barely missing a tip of one of the horns. Zankor's straps broke loose, and the pair tumbled onto the dusty surface of the alien desert.

Adam was still in his pilot seat, held in by a jammed safety harness. Zankor was free of his seat and now struggling with the straps holding his arms bound behind his back. He bore down and let out a fierce scream, straining his muscles until the already compromised strap broke away. He set to work freeing his ankles.

Adam was also at work trying to free himself from the restraints. The buckle was jammed, but the back of the seat was broken, with the right corner ripped by the bull's horn. Adam shoved at the shoulder straps, thankful now that they had been made for a much larger creature. He slipped a shoulder out from the strap and wiggled until the second one came through. He fell onto the ground just as Zankor released the bindings on his feet. He charged as only a bull could do, head down and horns swinging from side to side.

Adam was on his feet and sprinting away. It wasn't the manliest thing to do, but it worked. Zankor continued to chase after the Human until he realized he couldn't catch the fleet-footed alien. Besides, he was limping, having been injured in the crash.

After about five minutes, both parties stopped

about twenty feet away from each other, panting and aching from the crash. Adam hadn't had time to assess his own injuries but falling onto the soft clump of alien bull cushioned his fall. He was bruised, and his nose was bleeding, but that was about it. His body would heal miraculously fast, thanks to the slow-motion cloning it was going through. But for now, he seemed to be in better shape than his opponent.

Zankor turned back to the ruined copter and limped off toward it.

"Hey, hold up a minute," Adam said. "I'm not going to let you just walk away."

"Try to stop me."

Adam snorted. Had the cocky bastard forgotten about Adam's MK-88? And that's when Adam realized his weapon was missing, lost somewhere during the crash. Zankor was running again and with a sizeable head start. Whoever found the weapon first would control the game.

Adam ran off for the wreckage as well while having to circle around to get past Zankor. There was desperation in the bull's movements now, and he made it to the wreckage before Adam, but he still needed to find the gun.

Keeping Adam at bay with swipes from his deadly horns, Zankor rifled through the smashed cockpit. Adam kept making feints, trying to get into the cockpit himself. The Nefarean wasn't going to let that happen.

And then Zankor fell back and swung around in Adam's direction, the MK firmly in his grip. Adam couldn't tell what setting it was on, but the last time he'd used it, the weapon was set for stun. Now, he watched Zankor grin and level the MK at the Human.

And then came the pregnant pause as the targeting computer went through its locking phase. Adam had no choice. He couldn't assume the gun was still set on stun. Now, it was his turn to charge the bull.

Before the MK could lock on, Adam closed the gap and crashed a shoulder into the belly of the bull. To Zankor's shock, Adam was much heavier than he appeared, and he knocked the Nefarean into the broken cockpit while scrambling across his body to grasp the alien's gun hand with both of his. Not surprisingly, Adam was able to force the arm back with relative ease.

Zankor was surprised. He wasn't expecting Adam to be so strong, and when the Human twisted his wrists, the bull cried out in agony and released the weapon. Although disarmed, Zankor was still a deadly adversary. He rolled to his right, dislodging Adam, who landed in the dirt and then rolled away, barely avoiding the stabs the alien was making at him with his horns.

Finally, Adam regained his feet, and the pair of combatants faced off against one another, mano-to-alien.

Adam knew that Zankor's right leg was hurt, so

before the alien could catch his second wind, Adam struck. He dipped in low, using his smaller size as an advantage, sweeping the leg with one of his own. Zankor cried out in pain and fell on his side while Adam spun around and came at him from behind. He let loose with a flurry of quick fists to the bull's block head. As with aliens in the past, Adam had to pull back on the intensity of the blows to avoid shattering the alien's skull. The three million credits were for the return of the general to Nefar *alive*. Killing him would kill his bounty.

It took a combined eight punches before Zankor's arms fell to his side, and he stopped defending the hits. He was still conscious, but barely.

Adam rolled away before climbing to his feet and going back to the copter to get his gun. He checked the setting. To the alien's credit, he'd dialed the weapon all the way to Level-1, which was deadly, even to a Human if it hit in the right spot or was close enough. Adam smirked. All Zankor had to do was pull the damn trigger. Instead, out of habit, he relied on the targeting computer, and that cost him the victory.

Zankor was still sprawled out on the desert floor, his eyes closed and his face swollen. As Adam walked up to him, his bloodshot eyes opened, and he stretched out a painful grin.

"I congratulate you on your victory. Quite impressive."

"So, you concede? No more hijinks?"

"Hijinks did not translate, but I assume it means attempts to escape. I cannot promise that, but for the moment, I am pacified."

"Good; now, can you get to your feet?"

"I will try. Striking my right knee has made the injury even worse."

Zankor struggled to his feet, favoring his right leg.

"What now?"

Adam looked around at the expanse of open desert. There was nothing to see, no roads or other signs of civilization.

"We have to walk," he told his captive.

"I was unconscious for the start of our journey, but it appears we are south of Issennor and my camp. I assume you do not want to head in that direction. That would make the nearest settlement Yaz'in Calanet approximately ten standard miles to the south."

"What's there?"

Zankor grinned but then grimaced from his cut lips. "There is an aerial port there ... if that is your question. You can find a flight to Issennor."

"Do you have friends in Yaz'in, whatever you called it?"

"Would I tell you if I did?"

"I supposed not." Adam waved the MK-88 at Zankor. "We better get moving. Ten miles is a lot to cover with your bum leg before nightfall. Can you make it?"

"Will you carry me if I cannot?"

"For the three million credits they're offering for your return, I might consider it. Now ... *git along, little doggie.*"

Zankor frowned.

"Never mind," Adam said. "A feeble attempt at Human humor."

4

Zankor was moving along quite well, considering his injured leg. Even then, it would take all five hours of the remaining daylight for them to reach the town. Adam wasn't anxious to spend a night in the desert with the bull. Besides, at some point, the general's troops would widen the search, and if they found the wreckage of the quadcopter, footprints would lead them to Adam. Of course, neither of them had a good read on how far the town was. That depended on where the copter crashed.

"You are a Human," Zankor said after about an hour of walking in silence.

"That's right."

"I am a student of military history throughout the galaxy, and I have studied your species, as well as others of the major races; however, I have never met a Human before."

"Yeah, we're pretty rare these days."

"That is true. And now you are a fugitive recovery agent. How did that come to be?"

"I wasn't ready to go back to Earth with everyone else after the Klin invasion, and I needed work. It seemed like a natural fit."

"Indeed!" Zankor exclaimed. "I admit to embarrassed admiration for what you did to me, not only in your suppression of a much larger creature but for the courage—foolishness—to enter my camp to collect me. You are an intelligent creature; surely, you must have seen the insanity in the action."

"I might have reconsidered if your guard hadn't attacked me. After that, I didn't have much of a choice."

"You could have entered your vehicle and raced for Issennor. Instead, you did the opposite. A masterful strategic maneuver."

"But crazy," Adam conceded with a grin.

"Yes, and that was why it worked; it was so unexpected. Tell me your name, Human."

Adam grimaced. "I would prefer not to. It's something people in my profession don't advertise. They simply call me *The Human*."

"Understandable."

They walked in silence for a few more minutes before Zankor spoke again.

"I have had a theory for some time regarding the power structure in the galaxy, the galaxy prior to the Klin invasion. Would you care to indulge me?"

Adam had to admit it, but he was beginning to like the Nefarean. He was intelligent and polite to a fault and one hell of a fighter. That was Adam's kind of alien.

"Sure, go ahead."

"It has to do with the Humans, the Juireans and the original Klin. I understand the animosity that the Klin held toward the Juireans; they destroyed their homeworld and nearly killed off their race. Throughout the years, the Klin hid from the Juireans before resurfacing at the time of the Juirean-Human war. I do not think that was a coincidence. From my study of the times, I did not see a reason for the Humans and the Juireans to go to war. I believe the Klin were instrumental in that affair."

Adam raised his eyebrows. Being a Human—and who he was—Adam was more intimate with the details surrounding the war than probably anyone alive. That was why he found Zankor's question so odd. He assumed everyone knew the truth about what the Klin did. Obviously, that wasn't true.

"Your instincts are right, general—or do they call you Warden?"

"Warden is the official rank. But since you carry the weapon, you can call me whatever you wish."

Yep, he definitely was beginning to like the alien.

"Okay, Warden. For thousands of years, the Klin had been planning revenge against the Juireans, but they knew that they were far too weak of a species and too few in number to do anything on their own. So they recruited surrogate races to fight in their place. One of them was the Humans, and the other were the Kracori."

"I have heard of them, too," Zankor said. "But it is more in the context of the battle at the Dippean Void."

"It's pronounced Dysion. But you're right. I was there—"

"Surely, you are not truthful; you are too young."

Adam laughed. "Yeah, I get that a lot. But I'm older than I look."

"I was not aware Humans had the trait of longevity."

"Not all of us do. But I do. Now, back to the story. The Klin were abducting Humans and building an army they hoped could stand against the Juireans. Again, I was one of those they abducted. That's what got me into space in the first place. But then it got out that the Humans were planning to attack the Juireans —which we weren't. The Klin only made it seem like that so the Juireans would attack Earth. They did, but then the Klin and the army of what was called second-generation Humans counterattacked and wiped out the Juirean fleet. Still, we lost a couple of billion people in the attack. This made us mad, which is what the Klin wanted. Until then, most Humans didn't know anything about aliens. We didn't have star travel."

"You did not? How were you expected to fight the Juireans without such technology?"

"The Klin gave it to us and then set the Humans and Juireans at each other's throats, hoping we'd kill each other and leave them in charge of it all." Adam grinned a sad grin. "As I'm sure you're aware, we did a better job at fighting the Juireans than was expected."

"Yes, you won the war and eventually ruled the Expansion. But then you gave it up. Why?"

"We found out that ruling a galaxy is too big of a job for a single race. We found ourselves turning into the Juireans, and that was something we didn't want. So we put Kroekus in charge and went home to build a smaller empire in our part of the galaxy."

"Yes, I have read of Kroekus. He, too, disappeared suddenly."

Adam nodded. There was so much he wasn't telling the Nefarean; hell, he wouldn't believe it if he did. Even so, the conversation was resurrecting memories that Adam had tried to suppress. It seemed that in every major event that happened in the galaxy over the past forty years, Adam was part of it. How was that even possible? *The Human Chronicles*, as Adam often referred to that time in his life, was not only complicated, fortuitous and frankly unbelievable, but it was also exhausting just thinking about it. So much had happened, and not only that, but Adam was now into his second life, having died once and been cloned into a younger version of himself.

Suddenly, he was bone weary. Was he capable of living out a second life as eventful as the first? And if he was, did he even want to?

"It seems to me that the Humans never chose the path they are on," Zankor continued. "It was chosen for them, forced upon them by the Klin and others. How do you feel about that?"

"Angry," Adam admitted. "But in a way, relieved."

"Relieved?"

"What if all the weird shit that has happened in the galaxy over the past forty years still happened, and Earth became a victim of it instead of an active player? Would we have survived? I don't think so. First, there were the Juireans, then the Klin, then the Sol-Kor, the Nuoreans, the Mad Aris Kracion and then the New Klin. Surely one of those calamities would have consumed my planet and my race. But by being a part of it all, we were able to defend ourselves ... and others."

"For a simple recovery agent, you appear well-versed in the affairs of the galaxy. As the supreme military commander of my world, I am required to know my craft. I suspect you are more than you disclose. If I survive this ordeal, I shall have to spend more time studying the Human race. You appear much more nuanced than I first imagined."

Adam smiled. "That's us, an enigma needing solving. Believe me, for years I've tried to figure us out, and I can't. And I'm a Human. Perhaps looking at us with fresh eyes will produce some answers. Good luck with that."

"That is if I survive."

Adam snickered. "I imagine you'll come out just fine. People like you always do."

"Like me?"

"People in power."

Zankor nodded as he walked. "I had power at one time. But then I, along with many others, saw a flaw in our way of life and sought recourse. Dalin—the current leader of Nefar--discovered our discontent and launched a preemptive strike on us even before we acted."

"The warrant said you attempted a coup."

"An overthrow of the government, as per the translation? Nothing of the sort. We were preparing an opposition party for the coming elections. We never got the chance before Dalin declared us enemies of the state. Those he couldn't kill, he banished. I escaped with my life and a few of my loyal troops."

"Damn, that's not how it was made out to be."

Zankor laughed. "And now that you know the truth, you will surely set me free."

Adam grimaced. "I'm afraid not. I have a very stern Juirean boss who would not like it if I did."

"I was not serious … and you have a Juirean supervisor?"

"Yeah, funny how times change. He's actually a great guy and not your typical stiff-necked Juirean."

"Stiff-necked?"

"By the book, rigid."

"Such as I as a military commander."

"There are degrees. Regular Juireans are at one end of the scale; Tidus—my boss—is on the other end. His whole thing is about the credits. He doesn't care much what happens as long as he gets paid."

"Victory of a different kind; we are the same. And now, about letting me go…."

"Sorry, buddy, no can do. But hang in there. If this Dalin character is even halfway intelligent, he'll recognize what an asset he has in you. I'd rather try to sway you to my way of thinking rather than kill you. I'm sure you have followers. That would really piss them off."

Zankor frowned. "Do all Humans speak as you do, in strange word combinations and comparisons?"

"Most of us do; I know it really screws with the translators. See, I did it again. I'm sure *screw*s didn't come out the way I meant it."

"Thank you for saying that. It is a chore keeping up with your speech habits, if not your pace of walking. If it pleases you, may we slow some? My leg is hurting."

Yes, Adam really liked this alien. Too bad he had to turn him over to this Dalin character. But credits were credits, and Adam didn't do this job for his health. He was mercenary in that regard.

5

Suma Spanos had never been to the planet Nefar before. The farthest he'd traveled from Sandicor during his twenty-one standard years of life had been to the supply planets in the Ren-47 system. Sure, he'd seen videos of Nefar and the other Tier One worlds in the galaxy during his studies in school. But the real thing was much more intimidating.

The planet was modern in every respect, with technology to rival that of Formil or Juir. It was also a melting pot for beings within the Spur, and although Suma was raised among a plethora of alien species, he found the natives of Nefar to be especially strange and off-putting.

They were huge, muscular creatures with long horns and hooved feet on which they wore no shoes, and if it weren't for the adhesive pads they placed on the hard, yellowed soles, they would have made a horrendous clacking noise everywhere they went.

But it was their expansive horns that Suma couldn't draw his eyes from. The videos didn't do them justice, losing the scale when viewed on a tiny monitor. In-person, the horns created shivers running down the young miner's back.

Suma was a Zabbin, one of twenty-eight within the colony, all relatives of his. They had dark pink—almost red—skin and ear pads that covered the sides of their heads. The face was standard Prime, with a pair of grey eyes, nose holes and an almost square-shaped mouth. He stood just under seven feet tall, which made him a little shorter than a normal Zabbin. There was nothing physical about his body, meaning he had no special skin coating that would protect him against flash bolts or edged weapons. And he wasn't particularly strong.

Primarily, the Zabbin were known for their intelligence, which is why Suma worked with the data systems of the colony, which carried over into the wiring of electronic equipment, including power modules. He was also one of the specialists on Element-129, having concentrated his studies in school on the exotic material so vital to the survival of his community. He found it fascinating, an extremely rare, radioactive element that was used in the absorption blankets of various models of fusion reactors and fuel modules. It was the preferred material, although there was never enough for optimum use. Substitutes were used in about sixty-five percent of all applications; however, raw 129 demanded the highest price.

Even though Suma was the most knowledgeable about E-129, his naivety with the local terrain caused him to relegate command authority to Rilos A'hen. He was a much older and experienced miner, having traveled to Nefar many times to sell 129. He would lead the negotiations.

Rounding out the three-person delegation was Forlin Gann. He was along for his very basic knowledge of energy weapons; something passed down to him from his before-father. He was a Kandes Nan, and his family had immigrated to Sandicor only forty years before. The Kandes Nan had more experience with war, although it was now two generations removed. It was still more knowledge regarding weapons than any other colonist had, even though Forlin's was still second-hand. A survey of the three hundred colonists found that only seventeen had ever fired a bolt launcher before, and that was only at inanimate targets and for fun, never in anger or necessity.

Nefar was located four star systems from Minos, and during the trip, the trio discussed their mission. First, they had to sell the thirty-eight units of raw E-129 to get the credits—not only for weapons—but for a spare power module. They had none left, and if another failed, there would be no way to reboot the collector. Already short of credits to support the colony, the loss of any future harvest would be catastrophic. Suma was also taking Chanco at his word. If there was no future benefit in coming to Sandicor, he would strip the colony clean, leaving it with no means of survival. In a perverse way, the colony had to provide the raider with an incentive to keep coming back; otherwise, it would be their end.

Unless Suma and his team were successful in purchasing weapons for the colony's defense.

Through the use of the Galactic Library, Suma researched the cost of energy weapons for this region of the galaxy. With what they would make off the E-129 and taking into consideration the cost of a new power module and reserves for basic supplies before the next harvest, Suma figured they would have two thousand seven hundred energy credits available to buy the weapons. That should get them about a hundred basic MKs and twenty Xan-fi rifles, along with chargers for the power packs. That wasn't a lot, considering Chanco had over forty raiders, and they were much more experienced with their weapons than would be the colonists.

Suma reasoned it would have to be a surprise attack designed to shock the raiders and dispatch as many as possible before they could react. But Suma was also wise enough to realize that they would not kill all the raiders in one event. Some would survive, and that would be when the colonists would pay with their blood. But it would be worth it if it meant ridding the colony of Chanco once and for all.

However, the young miner's primary fear was that his fellow colonists would not have the courage to carry through with the plan. They said they would … but saying and doing were two different things. If they froze at the wrong time, that could mean the end of the colony prematurely, as Chanco would spare no one from his revenge.

But by then, Suma would undoubtedly be dead. Even so, he was already feeling guilty for what his actions were about to bring to the colonists. It was either win or lose; there was no other option.

The trio of miners had come to the capital city of Anacin to negotiate the sale of the E-129. It was a straightforward affair since the colony had been selling its element to representatives of Raynor for hundreds of years. But this time, they also went to Maris-Kliss, hoping to negotiate a higher price through competitive bidding. It worked, but only to the tune of five thousand additional credits, with Raynor still coming out the winner. The company representatives weren't happy with how the negotiations were handled, which could cost the colony in future transactions. But at this point, Suma and the others were only thinking about the immediate and not the future. They had other uses for the credits.

With credits in hand, Rilos led the team to the first advertised weapons dealer located only a few streets from the Raynor building. As they walked, Suma marveled at the towering structures and wide-open sky above. It was all so strange, so new and awe-inspiring.

The colony on Sandicor primarily existed in the Twilight Zone between hemispheres, where the temperature between the scorching hot starside and the land of frigid, perpetual night was moderated. Although the native atmosphere was toxic to living beings, the colonists built clear dome structures on the surface that afforded them the chance to gaze upon a semi-hospitable landscape while watching the glow of Minos and the star-filled black of night from the same vantage point. Even so, most of the life of a miner was spent underground in the ninety-plus miles of reclaimed lava tubes and caverns that were their home. Here, they'd carved out abodes, shops and offices, along with schools, playgrounds and entertainment venues. Each facility was limited, of course, since there were only three hundred permanent residents. But still, it made for a tight-knit and harmonious community of like-minded souls, even though they lived on one of the most dangerous planets in the galaxy.

As the miners entered the arms store, Forlin took point, approaching the counter and the purple-skinned, four-armed alien in attendance.

"I can be of service," the creature stated.

"We are here to buy energy weapons," Forlin said with confidence and a little too much bombast. The alien recoiled slightly.

"Of course; that is what we sell here, among a slim inventory of rare ballistic armament, even of Human origin."

The clerk seemed particularly proud of that last statement, although Suma did not know what a *Human* was.

"We are interested in Maris-Kliss models and even Xan-foo."

The clerk frowned. "You mean to say Xan-fi?"

"Yes, of course, Xan-fi," Forlin corrected himself.

Suma watched the purple creature stretch out a thin grin. Had Forlin made a mistake? Was he not as versed in the vernacular of weapons as he said?

The clerk withdrew a bolt launcher from a lower cabinet.

"This is the basic MK-88. It has a twenty-shot capacity at Level-1, forty at two and seventy at the stun setting. The battery can recharge in only forty standard minutes using the universal energy conversion chart. This is a used unit."

"What is the cost?"

"Three hundred forty EUs."

Suma grabbed Forlin by the arm and pulled him back. Rilos joined them.

"That is too expensive," Suma said in a panic.

"I agree," Rilos concurred. He worked a datapad. "With the extra five thousand credits we earned for the 129, we have seven thousand seven hundred to purchase weapons. At three hundred forty, we could only buy twenty-two units. That will not be enough."

"Yes, and I understand there are lower-rated models of the MK flash weapon," said Suma. "We do not need '88s."

"Is there an issue?" the clerk asked.

Suma turned to him. "We are only looking for the basic model. I believe it is the seventeen."

The alien frowned again. "MK-17s are rarely used these days. There are much more efficient weapons and with faster targeting computers. In reality, it is the onboard computer that is the most beneficial feature, and the '88 is top-rated in its class."

"We need a hundred weapons," Rilos explained, letting his age add credibility to the negotiations. It had worked with Raynor and MK; perhaps it will work here. "And we have a limited budget. For a bulk sale, what is the best price you can give us on a hundred 17s and twenty Xan-fi standards?"

The clerk recoiled. "A hundred units is not considered a bulk sale, but let me see what I can work out."

He operated a computer pad on the counter. "Of course, we have MK-17s in stock, and I could let you have them for one hundred fifty credits each. The Xan-fis are more expensive. They will be four hundred each. The total for your order will be twenty-three thousand credits plus the five percent licensing fee to the registry. That will be twenty-four thousand, one hundred fifty EUs. And all weapons sales are cash only."

The three miners stood in shock at the price. It was over three times the budget they had for the devices. If they spent twenty-four thousand on weapons, they could not afford a new power module. Either that or they'd have to forgo the supplies needed by the colony. Either way, it was one or the other, but not both, not if they spent twenty-four thousand on weapons. This was far beyond any of their expectations and magnitudes higher than what Suma had figured from his research on the Library.

"That is too much," he managed to mumble to the clerk.

The purple-skinned creature was unphased. "Then perhaps the number of units could be scaled back, or you go with either MKs or Xan-fis, but not both."

Suma was shaking his head. "That will not work. These weapons are for a specific purpose."

"Most are," said the clerk dryly.

"Is there not a less expensive bolt launcher available," Forlin asked.

"The Innis make a hand-held launcher, but the targeting computer is notoriously slow and inaccurate, and the Level-2 capacity is only eight bolts. And the charging time is two hours."

"What is the cost of those units?"

"Eighty credits."

Suma didn't need a datapad to work the numbers in his head. That was still eight thousand units … three hundred credits over their entire weapons budget. And they would have none of the longer-range, more powerful Xan-fis. And if they settled for inferior devices, that would mean additional casualties among the colonists when they confronted Chanco.

There was an awkward moment of silence before Rilos nodded to the clerk. "I thank you for your time, but it appears we have more calculations to work through. Perhaps we will return, but for now, we must go."

The purple alien smirked. He didn't appear too upset at losing the sale; perhaps he never believed the miners were true customers to begin with. Suma had to agree with him, to a degree. But Rilos was right; they had much to discuss. Perhaps it was the plan itself that needed shelving. Save the credits, go through a few more harvests, and then return when they have more.

But Chanco said he would not be as generous with

future harvests. Would there even be a surplus in the future, or would the colony have to suffer through even deeper reductions in essential supplies just to buy the weapons that could get them all killed?

As the trio stepped out onto the crowded street, Suma felt weak-kneed and ashamed. Had he miscalculated everything? Had he let his emotions cloud his judgment? He shook his head. He'd done his research. The Library had the price for MK-17s estimated to be thirty-five credits each. So, why was the clerk asking so much?

"He tried to take advantage of us," Rilos snarled to the others, answering Suma's unspoken question. "He saw the desperation in our faces. He also sensed we have more credits than we were willing to spend. He was shrewd, an experienced merchant."

"That does not help our situation," Forlin snapped. "I told you I had limited knowledge and none in acquiring weapons. I say we forget this misplaced quest and return to Sandicor. We have five thousand extra credits to buy supplies. That will make the colony happy."

"Five thousand?" Suma snapped. "What would we have if Chanco had not taken sixty units from us? How many supplies could we have bought with those credits? Five thousand is an insult."

"I agree … with both of you," Rilos said. "But now we are operating on emotion. Let us find an establishment for food and take our time figuring out what to do next. We are here on Nefar; let us not leave until we have examined all options."

The restaurant was very near the city center, where the tallest buildings could be viewed from a window booth. Suma tried to distract himself by gazing at the structures and marveling at their construction. On the opposite corner was the administrative center for the planet, a cluster of a dozen buildings or more where the government was housed. It made sense that the weapons dealer was located so close. Suma was sure the government was one of his best customers.

Which got Suma wondering. Perhaps it is the *location* that is dictating the high cost of the weapons. If they went to a far-off province, would they find lower prices? It could be the capital city that has inflated the prices as much as they appear to be.

Suma was the only one of the three whose mind was still working through the problem. The other two were busy discussing the menu on their computer screens. Each had the items detailed in their native language and was ecstatic about the myriad choices available to them. There were so many! There was very little variety on Sandicor, so this meal was becoming the highlight of their trip.

Suma was about to give in to his own rumbling stomach when he noticed a large transport pull up to the side of the government complex. He took notice because everyone on the street was watching the transport with an electric buzz moving through the population. All the horned natives stopped to stare as a smallish Prime exited the back seat of the vehicle holding a tan-colored strap. He pulled on it, and other creature emerged from the transport. It was one of the natives, an older specimen but just as large and deadly looking as all the others.

And then Suma noticed that the native had his arms shackled and a collar around his neck and was being led by the much smaller, pink-skinned alien. With a little flick on the leash, the Nefarean began walking toward the complex as a nervous crowd formed nearby. Even from where Suma sat, he could hear the rumblings of the natives. A few cheered, while most others stood in rapt silence or muttered to each in muffled conversations.

Soon, Rilos and Forlin also took notice of the disturbance across the street.

"What is happening?" Forlin asked.

Suma shrugged.

Just then, a Nefarean rushed into the restaurant and spoke to the employees.

"It is Warden Zankor! He has been captured."

"Captured?"

The native shook his big head, his deadly horns sweeping from side to side. "I, too, am confused."

"Who is that with him?" asked one of the servers.

"They say he is *The Human*."

"The recovery agent?"

"Yes; that is what they say."

Human, Suma thought. He'd just heard that word for the first time in the weapons store. Now, he heard it again. What is a *Human*?

The stunned crowd, both inside the restaurant and out, watched as *The Human* guided the massive Nefarean to the largest building. Even after the pair disappeared inside, the crowd remained, growing even larger as the minutes passed.

Suma took out his datapad and did a search, first for *recovery agent* and then for *The Human*. There were listings for both, although not much on *The Human* by himself, but a wealth of information about a race of beings called Humans. Suma had barely started reading when an idea formed in his head. He would discuss it with the others once he'd finished his research. But for the moment, he felt exhilarated. His dreams of ridding the colony of the Chanco menace weren't dead yet.

6

Adam was confused by the reaction of the crowd. A few cheered for the return of the fugitive military commander, but they were scattered and subdued. The bulk of the Nefareans were stunned. Did they fear for what Dalin would do to Zankor and what repercussions it would provoke? Adam didn't know. He'd already resigned himself to the fact that he was doing something he really didn't want to do but was obligated to finish. Zankor and the Nefareans had made their own bed. They would have to sleep in it, not Adam Cain.

Adam entered the main magistrate's office, causing a stir among the long-horned officials seated at their desks or manning counters. No one seemed anxious to approach the pair, leaving Adam standing awkwardly at a counter, waiting to be served.

Eventually, an aging female came up to Zankor, ignoring Adam.

"Warden Zankor, it is a pleasure to have you back. I have called Pep-Lead Filantis. He will be here presently to serve you." Then the female turned a scowling face at Adam. "Remove the shackles; they are not necessary."

Adam shrugged. She was right. Where could Zankor go now? He was in their custody; Adam had done his job.

He unlocked the wrist restraints and then the collar, letting the heavy metal clamps fall to the floor with a clatter.

"I am an employee of Starfire Security, and I remand the prisoner into your custody," Adam said formally. "At the same time, Starfire Security makes a formal claim for the bounty offered for his capture and return to Nefar as detailed in the Galactic Warrant Boards, file number GH-12957-NV-34."

The female again ignored Adam.

"I am very sorry for this crude treatment, Warden. All will be corrected once—yes, here comes the Pep-Lead."

"Warden Zankor," said a nervous-looking bull as he came from the back of the room. "I am surprised to see you … and under these conditions."

"Greetings, Filantis. It has been a while. And I, too, regret coming to you under these trying conditions."

A crowd had gathered, and the faces of these Nefareans appeared to convey more joy than anything else. *At last, the fugitive Zankor has been apprehended*, was how Adam read it.

Then Pep-Lead Filantis scowled at Adam for a moment before turning an embarrassed expression to the Warden.

"I sincerely apologize that the warrant was not lifted after the succession. It is understandable since we never imagined anyone would be fool enough to accept the contract. You were with over three thousand of your warriors. It would have been suicide to attempt your capture."

Zankor turned to Adam. "One would have thought so," he said sarcastically. "One would have been incorrect. Seemingly, my friend here has done the impossible, and I am now here to face the tribunal. Perhaps then I can plead my innocence without the fear of late-night reprisals."

"You appear confused, Warden," said Filantis, deep creases furrowing his prominent forehead. "You are no longer a fugitive. Only three days ago, Dalin Luz conceded his position. Your friend and associate Rosmin Ossin is now the Leader of Nefar, and technically, you are the Supreme Military Pep of the planet. Were you not made aware?"

A hard look came to Zankor's black eyes. "I only communicated with Nefar sporadically. I have not spoken with my contacts in five days. I must say, this news is sudden yet welcome. What has become of Dalin?"

"He and his family have left Nefar, along with many of his top associates. My friend Zankor, the planet is yours, along with your faction. I shall now be the first to congratulate you. The change has been welcomed across most providences, with more accepting the transition every day."

Adam listened to the exchange in stunned silence as a myriad of questions and realities swarmed through his head. If Zankor was no longer wanted, how would that affect the bounty? Will he even get paid? Hell, will he even make it off Nefar alive? He had manhandled the Supreme Military Leader of the planet. He'd even killed a soldier. Would he be the next to be placed in shackles and hauled away to a Nefarean prison, to spend the rest of his very long life in a cell literally smelling like bullshit?

He shifted in his stance, not wanting to appear weak and uncertain. He'd done the job as advertised. It wasn't his fault the situation at home changed.

"What about the bounty?" Adam asked the Pep-Lead. "I fulfilled the terms of the contract as specified at the time. I deserve to be paid."

Adam recoiled from the angry glares from the assembled mass of killer bulls. The silver tips of a dozen sets of sharpened horns reflected the light through the office windows and the overhead lights. It would be impossible to beat these odds. And he didn't even have his MK-hybrid; it was left downstairs at the security station. Adam Cain was completely at the mercy of the bulls. Perhaps he should have been nicer to Zankor…

The Pep-Lead turned his attention to Zankor. "Warden, I concede the decision to you. It was you who was led by a collar—as would a lowly animal—before the citizens outside and within the building, humiliated and shamed. I will accept whatever decision you make concerning this, this alien." The word *'alien'* was spoken with dripping venom.

Zankor turned to Adam and cast his dark orbs down at the diminutive creature, the creases on his face neutral and impossible to read. The moment dragged on for what seemed like an eternity, right up to the point where Adam was about to speak again to plead his innocence—

"Pay him."

"Very well, Warden," the Pep-Lead said quickly. He turned away to signal others in the room when he stopped and frowned. "Parden my understanding … did you say *pay* him?"

"I did," said Zankor loudly. And then a smile

stretched across his broad face. "This *alien* is called a Human. We have all heard of his race, even as few Nefareans understand the context. I, too, know very little about the Humans, but through my interaction with this individual, I have learned more. As you said, Filantis, you could not imagine a being foolish enough—or capable—of fulfilling the warrant contract. And yet *The Human* did, and against impossible odds. And throughout it all, he conducted himself with skill and professionalism. He did what he had to do; there was no humiliation, no overt cruelty. Because of that, he deserves the credits offered for my capture and return. So, Filantis, pay him his credits and allow him to leave the planet unmolested."

There was a moment of stunned silence before the Nefareans began to move again, albeit with restraint. Everyone had been frozen in place, waiting for Zankor's decree. When it came, it wasn't what was expected, but they honored it just the same. Zankor even offered his hand to Adam, helping instruct the alien on the proper backhand swipe that was a handshake on Nefar.

Adam was led to an office in an adjoining building where the three million energy credits were transferred to the Starfire Security account; they didn't make million credit payments in cash. That was fine. Adam didn't want to walk around with that much money on him anyway.

It would also make Tidus very happy to see three million credits appear in the business account. And Tidus checked the ledger at least three times a day.

7

By the time Adam left the administration complex, the word had circulated of Zankor's release, and the crowd had disbursed. Relieved, he hailed the first transport he found for the ride back to the spaceport and his waiting starship. But first, Adam hit the nearest bar outside the port compound. He needed a drink—several, in fact—to help calm his nerves.

Although the mission was a success, there was a moment when he genuinely feared for his life. Adam didn't like that feeling. He'd already died once, and that was enough as far as he was concerned.

The bar was what one would expect to find outside an intergalactic spaceport, somewhat dingy and filled with the purple haze of smokesticks, along with the customary pungent odor that came with a dozen alien species crammed into one room. There was squeaking in the background, which Adam recognized as alien music. He chose to tune it out and concentrate on getting drunk. The *Arieel* was only a short walk away, and with a nineteen-day journey back to Tel'oran, he'd have plenty of time to sleep off even the worst hangover.

As was his habit, Adam scanned the patrons for any obvious signs of hostility. It was rare, but it did happen. If it wasn't a grudge held against Humans in general, it might be personal. Adam had been kicking around these kinds of establishments long enough that occasionally he encountered a past *acquaintance* who was out to settle a score. As was said, it didn't happen often, but when it did, it generally didn't work out too well for the *acquaintance*.

But Nefar could be different. He'd just pissed off the majority of the planet by marching one of their global heroes down the road on a leash. Probably not his smartest move. Fortunately, there were no natives in the bar. That was good. Adam wasn't in the mood to tangle with any pair of two-foot-long horns this evening.

As he slipped into a booth and spun the blood sampling box around to him, he noticed that an alien at the bar was watching. The creature was slim and light-skinned with blond hair and very Human-like blue eyes. He noticed when Adam locked his attention on him and grinned, nodding slightly. Adam nodded back. Nothing there, just a couple of macho males acknowledging each other's presence.

Once his blood was sampled, the computer took over and displayed a menu of not only compatible intoxicants but also a full food menu. That was when it hit Adam that he hadn't eaten in hours. A full and decadent meal—decadent for the bar—was in order. Again, he'd have plenty of time to work it off on the way back to Tel'oran and Starfire Security. And unlike the past several times, Adam would be returning from a successful operation and after getting paid. That should go a long way toward healing the rift between him and Tidus. Things hadn't gone exactly according to plan recently. In spite of the shock from earlier today, this mission was one of his easiest.

The first helping of food and alcohol had come and gone, and Adam was still hungry and thirstier than when he arrived. He ordered a dessert and another stiff drink, and while he waited to be served, he began to groove a little to the scratchy alien music. *Not bad*, he thought. *A good beat; I could dance to it.*

Then, as he'd done with everyone who entered or left the bar over the past hour and a half, he noticed three assorted aliens come through the door and look around. Immediately on alert, Adam watched as they scanned the dim room, taking in each of the customers before their eyes locked on him. They weren't armed—

as far as he could tell—and they didn't have a look of either anger or serious intent. Instead, they looked nervous and out of place. *No threat here.*

But then they moved toward his table.

At least as a threat, the trio of aliens would have been interesting. As it was, Adam was annoyed even before they reached his table.

"Forgive," said a tan-skinned creature with huge, flat ears that flanked his roundish face. "We believe you to be the one known as *The Human*." He looked over at his two companions quickly and then back at Adam. "We witnessed your arrival at the governmental complex earlier today. We wish a moment of your time to discuss a business proposal."

Adam scanned the faces of the aliens. Big Ears had a harmless demeanor, as did the smaller, green-skinned being who kept shifting his eyes from side to side nervously, concerned more about the bar than Adam. The third member was different. He was older and harder looking, with yellow skin and the remains of an angry scar lancing across his prominent forehead. Adam focused on him, trying to imagine the fight that had given him the scar. The fact that he was standing in front of Adam meant he'd been victorious. This was someone to watch.

"I'm sorry, but I don't take freelance work. You'll have to go through my employer. It's Starfire Security. They're in the Library."

Adam was proud of himself. Over the past six months, he'd been more than willing to take on side work, a practice that had not only bankrupted him but almost got him fired from Starfire. He'd learned his lesson. He had a good thing going with Tidus, and he didn't want to fuck it up ... not again.

Besides, he had one-point-six million energy credits stashed away on Tel'oran, plus his share of the three million the Nefareans had just paid Starfire. He was flush with cash and didn't need side work.

"That is understandable," Big Ears began, "however, this will only take a moment of your time to present our offer. For the honor, we will pay for your meal and—" The alien looked at the collection of three empty beverage glasses on the table—"well, for your meal."

Adam had enough alcohol coursing through his bloodstream that he laughed. Paying for his drinks *could* get pricy. This told him these guys were on a budget. But Adam was also feeling gregarious. He waved a hand at the seat cushions.

"Please, take a seat. If you're paying, I'm listening, but no guarantees. What can I do for you?"

The three aliens scooted into the booth on both sides of Adam, with Scarface seated by himself to Adam's right.

"I am called Suma," said Big Ears. *Dammit*, Adam thought. He liked calling the alien Big Ears. Now he winced, knowing that Scarface also had a name. Even so, he would continue to call him Scarface. It was too cool to pass up.

"And this is Forlin," Suma continued, indicating the green-skinned creature next to him. "And across the table is Rilos."

Adam locked eyes with Scarface—Rilos—who quickly looked away. *Okay, not so much a threat.*

"And you are?" Suma asked.

Adam motioned with his fingers. "Human, just call me the Human; everyone does."

"Very well, kac-Human."

Nearly every race had their substitutes for Mister or Miss. Suma's appeared to be *kac*.

"So, what do you need?" Adam asked. The server had just brought his next beverage and then asked the aliens if they needed service. All three declined, although the one called Forlin looked as if he wanted to order but was shut down by stern looks from the others.

"First, you must understand our situation. It will help with your consideration of our offer. We are miners from the planet Sandicor. It is not far from here. We live mainly in tunnels under the surface of a world where one side continuously faces our star while the other side is in constant darkness. Our colony is small but close and respectful, although life on Sandicor is not easy."

"What do you mine?"

"It is ejecta from the star Minos, and in particular, a material called Element-129. It is very rare and is used in fusion reactors."

Adam shrugged. He'd never heard of Element-129; in fact, with what little he knew of the periodic table, he didn't even know it went up that high. But this was outer space … and aliens. They were literally light-years ahead of Humans when it came to stuff like that.

"All right," Adam said. "You guys are hardworking and honest, but something is bothering you."

"That is true!" said Suma ecstatically. "You are very perceptive. To further explain, the harvests of E-129 come in waves, and we work very hard to collect what we can. Even so, it is barely enough to sustain the colony. Recently—over the past four standard years—a bandit by the name of Chanco Kantos has been coming to Sandicor and robbing us of not only a large portion of our 129 harvests but other valuables as well. He and his raiders are causing incredible hardship for the colony, turning a once prosperous and content community into one of pain and despair."

Suma took a break to look at his companions as Adam drained another drink and signaled for another. He was also munching on his dessert while half listening to the alien's story.

"Go on; I'm listening."

Suma watched Adam as he stuffed a crusted breadstick in his mouth, aghast at how much of it he was able to get inside. Then he continued. "The situation on Sandicor has gotten so bad that a consensus was reached. We are determined to do something to stop Chanco. Rilos, Forlin and I have come to Nefar to sell what little E-129 Chanco allowed us to keep from the last harvest. We have also come to purchase weapons, weapons for which to defend our colony against outside threats. However, we have run into an obstacle. We believe the merchants are overcharging, and they do not respect us as viable customers. That is why we have come to you."

Adam recoiled. "I'm not a weapons dealer. I don't have anything to sell you. That's not my business."

"We realize that. What we request from you is that you act as our purchasing agent. You will command more respect and help negotiate a more reasonable price."

"What are you looking for?"

"MK-17s and Xan-fi long-range bolt launchers."

Adam nodded. The standards. "What kind of quotes have you been getting?"

"One hundred fifty for the 17s and four hundred for the Xan-fis. According to my research on the Library, those prices are wildly out of order."

Adam puffed out his cheeks, expelling a tiny piece of the breadstick. "You can say that again. That's highway robbery. You're getting those prices here in Anacin?"

"That is correct, although, I must admit, we have only been to one dealer."

"That probably doesn't matter," Adam said. "In town, the prices are all going to be about the same. But I agree with you; that's way too much."

Suma beamed at his companions. "I told you as much. They did not believe that my estimates were correct. They thought I had made a mistake."

"You did ... for Nefar. You might try over on Calamont. They were a big arms supplier before the Klin invasion. They have a surplus of old MKs."

"Where is Calamont?" Scarface asked, speaking for the first time. "We are not familiar with other worlds in the Spur except those within a few light-years of Sandicor."

"Calamont is about sixty light-years from here."

Scarface grimaced. "We do not have a vessel that can make that journey. Is there nothing you can do here on Nefar to help us?"

Adam shook his head. "This is a hub planet for the region. They get a lot of traffic through here, so they can demand the highest prices. You know, supply and demand."

Adam felt like shit watching the spirit drain from the faces of the three aliens. They were defeated, and somehow, Adam felt responsible. Hell, all he'd done was tell them the truth.

"Hey, I'm sorry, but you can't fight reality. If you want to buy weapons on Nefar, you have to pay Nefar prices." And then Adam snickered. "But if I could get one-fifty for an MK and four hundred for a Xan-fi, I might have a couple back at my ship I could sell you. I could buy four of each back on Tel'oran for what you'd pay me for one."

That didn't help the mood.

"Four weapons would not help. We need much more," said the alien called Forlin.

"How big of a gang does this Chanco character have?"

"Forty or more," Suma answered. "And they have weapons, lots of weapons."

"It's probably good then that you guys can't buy enough guns. Going up against an army of raiders that big, without the right skills and equipment, will only get you kill—"

Adam stopped speaking as he saw the three aliens turn pale for their respective skin colors. They were focused on the door and the four creatures who had just entered. Adam had been lax in his observations, perhaps lulled into a false sense of security by the liquor and the conversation and didn't see them come in. Now he focused on the newcomers, seeing that they had all the makings of some tough hombres.

"Friends of yours?" Adam asked.

"It is four of Chanco's raiders," Suma replied.

"Including Vor, one of his lieutenants," Forlin added. "Perhaps they will not recognize us—"

But it was too late. The four raiders had also made the customary sweep of the room, gauging threats, when their eyes fell upon the miners. A tall, yellow-skinned creature grinned and motioned for the others to follow. This must be the one called Vor, Adam reasoned.

"What are they doing here?" Adam asked, but the miners didn't have a chance—or the ability—to answer before the raiders were hovering next to the table.

"You are the troublemaker called Suma," Vor stated. "What are you doing here? You are supposed to be on Sandicor, suckling your young and sulking over your lost harvest."

"We have come to sell the E-129 Chanco left for us," Suma replied sheepishly. "You must know this is where we come to do it."

Vor snorted. "I do not trouble myself with the habits of your kind. All I know is that I cannot stand the vile stench of you underground vermin. Do you not have water on Sandicor? Do you not bathe to wash away the smell."

"It is the smell of fear, Vor," said another of the raiders. "That does not wash off."

Vor slapped the raider across the shoulder, and all

four of them burst into laughter. Adam could tell they were already drunk before they came into the bar. A history with the miners—combined with intoxicants—and the scene could turn violent at the drop of a hat.

"Hey, why don't you guys move on and take your drinks at the bar. No one is looking for trouble."

Vor locked his laser-like gaze upon Adam as the crooked grin on his face vanished. "Who are you to tell me what to do? Indeed, *who* are you? I do not recognize you from the colony."

"He is not of the colony," Suma said. "He is a friend we were having a meal with."

"A friend?" Vor questioned.

"Not really friends, more like acquaintances," Adam corrected. "In fact, we just met tonight."

Vor looked Adam up and down and, as with most aliens, saw his short stature and slim build as a weakness, not an advantage. "You have picked the wrong acquaintances. When you run with the vermin, you shall be treated as vermin."

Vor took Rilos/Scarface by the shirt and pulled him from the booth. Then he turned to Adam, ready to drag him from his seat as well. Just then, another of the raiders leaned over to Vor and spoke into his ear. The raider stopped, listened and then looked hard at Adam once again.

"Are you sure?" Vor asked his companion.

"Yes, I saw him myself."

"Dacis says you are the one known as *The Human* who single-handedly brought in Warden Zankor. However, I see you here, and I believe he must be mistaken. You are much too small to be a warrior of such reputation."

Adam leaned back in the booth, with his left arm draped over the back cushion and his right hand under the table and squeezing the grip of his MK-88 hybrid. From feel, he switched the weapon from energy to ballistics. Letting the aliens hear the full-throated blast from a 45-caliber round would help drive the point home that Adam wasn't someone to be trifled with.

But then Vor backed off.

"But I do not have to prove myself to you. You are at a table with losers, with the lowest of animal. That makes you no better than them, no matter what Dacis says you did earlier."

"You don't believe him?" Adam asked with a sinister grin. He was just drunk enough that taking out these four assholes would be the highlight of his mission. After all, he'd only killed one Nefarean so far. That was far below his average in alien kills. It would be almost sacrilegious for him to return to Tel'oran without at least some collateral damage. "Perhaps we should step outside then and let me give you a demonstration."

"Come, Vor," Dacis said, tugging at the arm of the senior raider. "We have come to Anacin to sell the 129, just as they have. But we have so much more. For now, we are wealthy. Let us enjoy our spoils while Suma and the others wallow in their loss. Let them return to Sandicor so they can collect more E-129 for us. They are so good at it."

"And we are good at taking it from them!" Vor laughed, turning away. "Yes, let us celebrate our good fortune." As he walked away, he turned his head back to Adam's table. "Now, run, little vermin. Go back to your tunnels. Work hard … and make us rich!"

They didn't stay in the bar. Dacis guided them through the door and into the night, where they would find a more hospitable establishment, which were plentiful outside the gates of the spaceport.

Adam released the MK and placed his hands on the table. He felt cheated but wasn't going to go out of his way to make a scene, any more than had already been made. He looked at the bar and noticed the blond-haired alien was no longer there. He wondered if he stuck around long enough to watch the confrontation with the raiders.

He turned his attention back to the miners.

"Well, that was interesting … and informative."

"How so?" Suma asked.

"It told me that if you did buy weapons to fight the bandits, you'd all end up dead. It takes more than weapons to fight people like that. It takes a savageness I don't think you have. You will have to be ready to kill and then kill some more. And then keep on killing until the threat is neutralized. Can you do that, Suma? Can the rest of your colony?"

"We will fight to save our homes and families, as would all living creatures."

"That's easy for you to say. Let me ask you: Would you have killed Vor tonight if you had the weapons? Again, I don't think you could do it."

"Let us be the judge of that. When necessary, we will fight."

"The necessity to kill can spring up at any time—"

"Will you help us buy weapons or not?" Suma growled. *The kid has spunk,* Adam had to admit. But confusing impatience for courage could prove deadly.

Adam shook his head. "All I would be doing is signing your death warrant. Honestly, you don't need weapons. What you need is an army of your own against people like Chanco and Vor. That's the only way this will work out for you."

"An army?" Forlin asked.

"Yeah, you know, mercenaries. Trained killers for hire."

"Will you be that army?" Forlin asked. "Or the start of one? And we can pay you."

Adam had already made up his mind not to help the miners. But still, he was curious to see how far they would go to hasten the death of their colony.

"How much can you pay for mercenaries?"

"We have almost eight thousand."

"Eight *hundred* thousand?"

"No, eight thousand."

Adam leaned back and placed his arms on the back cushions, a silly grin on his face. "Are you serious? Eight thousand credits are all you have? I see now why you're having trouble buying guns. Eight thousand wouldn't even pay for a fuel pod for my ship. And you expect to fight off Chanco with only eight thousand credits." He reached over and patted Suma on the shoulder. "Trying to fight a war on a budget will only lead to defeat. Give up on this crazy idea of yours. Go home. Go back to your planet and continue to live another day. It may not be a good life, but at least you'll have one."

Suma's face was a study of anger and frustration. Even so, the miners didn't have enough money to cause too much trouble for themselves. Without weapons, or a mercenary army in their stead, all the miners could do was tolerate the cruel reality of life. But, as Adam said, at least they'd have a life.

"I respect you for your honest assessment," Suma grunted. "However, we are not ready to give up. Our ship is in space seventy-four if you have a change of mind. We leave in two days."

"I leave tomorrow."

"In that case, please do not delay in reconsidering our proposal. We are serious about our needs. And we need your help more than you can possibly imagine."

And then the miners left the bar. Adam left a few minutes later after he settled up his account—his full account. The miners didn't pay for his food.

8

It was a pleasant night in the city of Anacin, with a moonless sky and a shroud of twinkling stars to light his way back to the *Arieel*. Adam was tipsy, but the evening's festivities had sobered him up more than he wanted. He was bloated from all the food and drink and felt cheated out of the long-term buzz he'd been hoping for.

But Adam didn't get a chance to wallow too long in his regret, not when he suddenly found himself on the ground and being pummeled by a trio of Vor's bandits from the bar. The fact that he was sober enough to notice that Vor wasn't among his assailants pissed him off even more than the beating he was taking. What a waste of good liquor.

With that thought out of his mind, Adam began to

concentrate on the fight, a fight in which he was the guest of honor. The three aliens were having a field day striking his head and body with the most powerful blows they could muster, which wasn't much by Human standards. And when Adam laughed, it only made the raiders angrier and more determined to cause him pain.

Typically, something like this would hurt a Human, but Adam wasn't a typical Human. And now the alcohol was mixing with his instinctive cloning reaction to bodily damage to heal his body almost as soon as an injury was inflicted. This was adequate for the level of trauma he was experiencing, the result of flesh-on-flesh hits, but it wouldn't protect him against more aggressive injury once the aliens realized it would take more than fists to take Adam out.

So, after a few moments of letting the raiders have their way with him, Adam went on the offensive.

By now, Dacis and the others were growing tired. They were drunker than Adam and thought they had more stamina than they did. To Adam, this was becoming a rope-a-dope strategy, but with him on the ground rather than against the ropes in a boxing ring.

With a clarity of mind that he shouldn't have, Adam sighted his first target. It was a barrel-chested alien who wound up and delivered a crushing blow to Adam's left temple while also dropping his guard and leaving his face an open target for Adam's right jab. It usually only took one unblocked punch to take out an alien, and that was the case here. Bone and cartilage shattered, and the raider's eyes rolled back in his head as he toppled over. It wasn't a knockout blow; it was a killer punch.

With Adam answering their attack, the other two aliens became more cautious. They climbed off of him and stood back, allowing Adam to get to his feet. They looked nervously at their dead companion, knowing he'd been taken out by one short yet solid punch.

"Okay, boys," Adam announced. "Let's play!"

And then he attacked, closing the gap between him and Dacis in the blink of an eye, faster than the bandit was expecting. Adam didn't bother with hitting him. Instead, he crashed into the body and threw Dacis back with an extension of his arms. In the light gravity of Nefar and with his thin bone structure, the alien went sailing, landing ten feet away and with an awful groan. He wasn't terribly injured, but he was out of the fight for a few seconds, enough time for Adam to concentrate on assailant number three.

This dude was bigger than the others, with forearms eighteen inches in circumference and a body that towered eight feet tall. Standing toe to toe, six-foot-tall Adam Cain could barely reach the alien's chin. Gathering his courage, the giant assessed the situation, believing he still had the advantage. He reached out with his four-foot-long arms and jabbed at Adam, keeping him at bay as he began to dance around. Adam was impressed with the footwork; apparently, so was the alien. He smiled at Adam, displaying a full set of black and yellow teeth, an obvious death challenge if Adam ever saw one.

Okay, if you insist, Adam thought. He mirrored the smile, although Adam's teeth were white and straight, the product of good dental hygiene as a child.

Adam swept aside the next jab and then moved in, landing a kick to the alien's side, about mid-torso. The monster felt it and backed farther away. But Adam didn't give him time to recover. He slipped in again under a defensive jab and executed a sloppy spin kick, sloppy because Adam was drunk. This one landed in the alien's gut, knocking the air from his lungs. Even for an awkward kick, it still felt as if the alien had been hit with a baseball bat if he knew what a baseball bat was. It stunned him long enough for Adam to make a short leap up to eye level and deliver a smashing right cross on the creature's chin.

To his credit, the beast didn't go down, but he should have. Instead, he staggered, with his long arms falling to his side and leaving his head undefended. This was when Adam delivered a carry-through uppercut that snapped the creature's head back so violently that it snapped his neck. He was dead before he timbered backward to the ground.

Dacis was now on his feet and with his MK out of its holster. The weapon was leveled, but the alien had yet to finger the trigger, knowing that the targeting computer would have trouble deciphering Adam from the other raider in the dim light outside the bar. But the big beast was now on the ground, and Dacis had a clear shot.

Adam normally didn't fear MK flash bolts, even if they were at Level-1. His superior healing abilities made him impervious even to that intensity of a shot unless it struck him in the head and at point-blank range. Even so, Adam didn't feel like getting shot this evening. The damn things stung like a bitch. So, he tumbled forward, rolling over and coming to his feet again before shifting to his right. Dacis did his best to keep the MK pointed at Adam but was having difficulty. And with each movement, Adam got closer to his target.

Growing tired and dizzy, Adam was out of patience with the alien. Although Dacis had been the only raider with any sense, Adam had to eliminate the threat and permanently.

A lightning-quick slap of his wrist knocked the MK from Dacis' hand, followed by a turn that brought Adam within the alien's arm reach. Continuing with his spin, Adam lifted his elbow and sent it crashing into the alien's neck; Dacis was too tall for it to reach his head. But the neck was good enough. His spine snapped, and his windpipe compressed. The alien slumped to his knees, gasping for breath and twitching from the spinal cord injury. He fell forward and continued to twitch, still alive, but only for the moment.

That felt good! Adam thought. *Three dead; not much of a score, but there weren't that many—*

A squeal rose up behind Adam, sending him spinning from instinct to face the unseen enemy. What he saw made him freeze in his tracks.

It was Vor, standing about fifteen feet away in the darkness and holding Adam's hybrid MK-88. For confirmation, Adam slapped the empty holster on his hip. Yes, it was his weapon; he'd lost it—again—just as he'd done with Zankor four days earlier. He really had to be more careful—

"This is a strange weapon you have and heavier than most."

"Then maybe you should put it down before you hurt yourself." Adam grimaced the moment he finished the line. It didn't pay to insult someone pointing a weapon at you, especially a weapon that had last been set on the 45-caliber ballistic setting. Adam wasn't immune to lead, not in the least.

Vor snarled at him while lifting the weapon a

couple of inches higher but still pointed squarely at Adam.

"I also see it has no targeting function. So, I just pulled the trigger? That, too, would be strange, but at this distance, I do not need a targeting computer."

The alien was catching on, which caused Adam to sober up completely. Any second now could be his last.

Just then, a blur zipped into Adam's field of vision from his right. It was so fast that Adam couldn't tell what it was, but whatever it was, it wrapped itself around the MK-88 and yanked it out of Vor's hand. The weapon went tumbling away until it crashed into the side of the bar with a thud.

Vor turned to his left, trying to make out where the thin green cord had come from. Adam looked too.

And then the thin, blond stranger from the bar stepped out of the shadows and into the dim light. He grinned at Adam and then turned to face Vor. The drunk bandit cried out in anger, upset that he'd been robbed of his chance to kill *The Human*. He took a step toward the blond alien. What Adam saw next was a shock, not only to him but to Vor as well.

A green tongue shot out of the alien's mouth, snaking out at blinding speed before impacting Vor's flat nose. It hit with speed and power, lashing across twelve feet or more, and delivered a near-knockout blow. Vor staggered back, his nose bleeding and his eyes watering. He hadn't recovered when the tongue sprang out again, this time wrapping around Vor's thick neck and tightening in a heartbeat. It was like a garrote, slicing through skin and producing a ring of gushing blood. The tongue didn't decapitate the raider; instead, it stopped tightening when it reached the neck bone, but it was enough to kill Vor on the spot.

The blond stranger stepped up to his victim, retracted his impossibly long tongue and then turned to Adam, smacking his lips.

"Yum, that is some tasty blood. And just the right amount of salt."

Adam stood his ground, still not sure whether the stranger was friend or foe. After a moment, Long-Tongue motioned toward the wall of the bar. "You should retrieve your weapon. After that, we will hide the bodies. There are trash receptacles around the back."

"Okay, fine," Adam mumbled. He stepped over to his MK and held it in his hand for a moment before slipping it into the holster. Long-Tongue was already dragging Vor around the corner of the bar. Adam took Dacis and joined him. In silence, the pair placed the four bodies into standard-looking dumpsters before walking back to the front of the bar.

"Can I buy you a drink?" Adam asked. "I feel I owe you something for saving my life."

The stranger laughed. "From the look of things, I do not believe you were in much danger."

Adam snorted. "That's where you're wrong. But that aside, *I* need a drink. Will you join me?"

"That I will."

They reentered the tavern as nonchalantly as possible and made their way to the bar.

"I'm Adam. Thanks again for helping me out. It wasn't your fight."

"So, *The Human* has a primary name. I shall make a note of that."

"You know who I am?"

"After today, I am sure most of Nefar knows who you are. I am called Vinset. I am honored to make your acquaintance."

The pair went through the blood-sampling routine before two drinks were deposited in front of them. Adam lifted his glass in a toast; Vinset was confused.

"A gesture of thanks and respect where I come from. It is called a toast."

"Then I will return the toast." Vinset lifted his glass, and Adam clanked them together.

"So," Adam began, "did you see the little confrontation I had with those four earlier?"

"I saw enough. If I am not mistaken, they are members of Chanco's tribe."

"You've heard of him—Chanco?"

"Yes; he keeps his main base at a town about two hundred miles from here. It is not a large village, but he controls it like a prison. I went there a week ago, looking for work."

"You went to Chanco to become a bandit, a raider?"

"I just knew he was looking for soldiers. I have been stranded on Nefar for a few months and was desperate to make some credits so I can leave."

"What happened? You obviously have skills he could use."

"As you have inferred, when I discovered that he ran his tribe as thieves and killers, I decided to look for more traditional employment. I saw you at the city center today. I have made fugitive recovery in the past. I query whether your company might be hiring?"

"It's not my company, but I'd be glad to put in a good word for you. But we usually require that you have your own starship. I take it you don't have one."

"I did when I came to Nefar."

"What happened to it?"

"A *triple burst* against a *long slide* ... that is what happened."

Adam frowned, not understanding.

"It is an unbelievable combination of Rassin hands that went in favor of my opponent."

Adam laughed. "You lost it in a card game?"

"It was only the last in a series of unfortunate card games. Lately, my luck has not been that good."

Adam lifted his glass and toasted again. "Join the club, brother; neither has mine."

"Do all Humans speak as you? I have never met one before."

"We're a strange group, but if you hang around us for a while, you'll get used to the way we talk."

Vinset finished his drink.

"What was it that caused the incident with the raiders? They appeared intent on disrupting your party."

"It wasn't a party. Those three seated with me are miners who have had their colony raided by Chanco. They mine something called E-129, and Chanco has been stealing most of it from them and barely leaving them enough to live on."

Vinset looked impressed. "One-twenty-nine is a very rare and expensive commodity. It is usually created in huge reactors run by the big energy companies, but even they cannot keep up with demand now that the galaxy is recovering after the Klin invasion. That is unfortunate for the miners. They could be in a very good position to earn substantial credits from E-129 if Chanco would leave them be."

"That's what the miners think. That's why they wanted me to buy them guns, so they can defend themselves."

"Against Chanco?" Vinset asked incredulously. "I

hope you did not agree. The raider tribe is vicious and skilled. Amateurs cannot stand against them."

"That's what I told them. So now they want to hire mercenaries."

Vinset's eyes got larger. "Mercenaries? How many … and how much?"

Adam waved his hand at Vinset. "Relax; they couldn't afford you."

"Be not so sure. My services come cheap, considering my present situation."

"They only have eight thousand credits for the whole force."

"A small band of experienced fighters could send a significant message to Chanco, enough to spare the miners for a while. And at the moment, even my share of eight thousand credits would be enough to get me to Tactori or even Jax. Are you joining the miners?"

Adam laughed. "You know what, before I left the bar the first time, I was dead set against it. But after what Vor and his people did to me outside, I may change my mind."

"You should!" Vinset exclaimed. "I have seen you fight, and I have heard the stories. You are worth any ten normal fighters. And I, well, I have more skills than simply my tongue." Then Vinset lowered his eyes. "But I understand that you could command a much higher price than the miners can afford. You are paid for what you are worth."

"Normally, I'd say you're right. But I'm currently between assignments, and I owe Chanco a little payback. I may do this job for free just to maintain my quota."

"Your quota?"

"My score of dead aliens and collateral damage."

Vinset grinned and nodded. "Of course, I understand. As I have said, I have heard the stories."

9

Suma and the others were ecstatic when Adam and Vinset arrived at their starship the next morning with the news that they'd help, even more so when it was learned they were coming as mercenaries.

"This doesn't mean we're going to do all the fighting," Adam explained. "We'll train you and set up the defenses. But even five or six mercs won't be enough to stop Chanco. You're going to have to help."

"Of course! It is what we were expecting from the beginning!"

The young miner was literally bouncing in his seat, even as the other two remained more subdued. In their eyes, Adam could see doubt … and fear. This was going to happen, and whatever reaction Chanco would have to their actions was something they would have to live—or die—with. Talk was one thing, but this was becoming far too real.

"But how will we pay you?" Rilos asked. "Any amount above eight thousand will come from supplies, and that set aside for the energy module."

"I'll do the job for free, and Vinset will accept two thousand." Adam saw the long-tongued alien perk up. He was expecting to make half that. "All together, we believe you can afford five to six mercs for your eight thousand. That's not much, but with your help, it will be enough to bloody Chanco's nose so that he'll leave you alone."

"I thought we were going to kill him?" Forlin asked. "Why would a simple bloody nose stop him from coming back? It will heal."

"It's a figure of speech," Adam explained wearily. It was like this nearly every time he opened his mouth around aliens.

"Where will we find the other mercenaries?" Suma asked. "The next flare is due in less than a month, and Chanco will know when it erupts. There seems to be much to do, and we know not where to look for warriors."

"Our friend Vinset has been on Nefar for a while, and he's had contact with a few skilled fighters like him. We'll start there. But something you have to accept: We still need credits for the weapons, maybe five thousand. As Vinset talks with his friends, I'll shoot over to Calamont and see what I can pick up. Your colony has no weapons of its own?"

"We took a count before we left. Twenty-nine is all we possess, and none of us is skilled in their use."

"We will train you," Vinset said. "But success will depend on surprise. Chanco must not know what you are planning. Can your people be trusted?"

"For three hundred years, our ancestors and families have lived on Sandicor. Together, we are more like a family than a community. And when one suffers, we all suffer. I will be honest; not all are enthusiastic about this path we are on. But all will do their part when the time comes. As we say, *the colony lives and dies together by the grace of Minos and the spirit of our souls.*"

Adam grimaced. "Well, Suma, that sentiment will soon be tested."

His name was Raccs, but the creature facing him did not care. All he was concerned with was the two hundred credits on the table and who would walk away with it victoriously.

The contest was simple ... and with edged weapons. The target was a knot in a vertical support beam about thirty feet away. The slender, fluid-armed being named Dok weighed the knife, bouncing it in his hand before turning toward the beam. His race was known for their prowess with blades, but he didn't advertise that fact as he maneuvered Raccs into the contest. This was how Dok made his modest living, and two hundred EUs would be a good start to his day.

Dok didn't care who went first; either way had its advantages. If he started the contest by striking the target dead center, then it would add pressure to his opponent, making him nervous. If he went second, then he would know what he had to do to win, so he didn't always go for the center. If he did, the word would get out, and he'd find no challengers. He was first in this contest.

With an anxious crowd cheering him on, Dok squared up on the target. He feinted with his first throw, appearing to have second thoughts. It was all part of the act, making it look as though the center strike would be luck rather than skill. But soon, the blade was twisting in the air and, as predicted, found its mark in the center of the dark red knot, vibrating for a few seconds before settling down.

The crowd went wild. Within the bar, there were a lot more than two hundred credits riding on the contest, and the good money was on Raccs. He was twice the bulk of Dok, with bulging muscles and dark, steely eyes. He had the look of a warrior, one who would know how to use throwing blades. Dok did not, which is why he was getting such good odds. A few of his surrogates circulated in the crowd, taking bets for him. It was easy money, especially when one already knew the outcome.

Raccs grunted and stepped up to the line. He cast an evil eye at Dok, his look accusatory and suspicious.

Dok shrugged meekly. "Fortune shines on me this day, it would appear."

Again, Raccs grunted.

Then he looked down at the tiny knife in his hand. It looked like a child's toy and not a real weapon. So, he tossed it aside and reached behind his back and withdrew the two-foot-long curved battle ax that was his weapon of choice.

Dok opened his mouth to protest but quickly shut it when Raccs glared at him. His blade was center target; there was nothing Raccs could do to beat him. He gestured for his opponent to continue.

Raccs grinned, and then having barely time to sight the target, he spun around and lobbed the battle ax across the room. From tiny tubes cut in the handle, the weapon whistled as it flew before impacting the foot-wide wooden beam directly on the prominent knot. But rather than embedding itself in the wood, it continued through, splitting the hardened material as if it was made of water. The beam shattered, cascading apart to either side as the ceiling slumped a few inches before stopping, dust drifting down on the now silent crowd.

Raccs turned to an equally stunned Dok, the silly grin still on his wide mouth.

"I win."

Dok began shaking his head. "No, you cannot. My throw was the best that could be made. At best, it is an equality."

"No, I win."

Dok looked to the crowd for support, but no one—not even the losers in the betting pool—was willing to side with him, not against the feeble-minded giant. He looked again at Raccs, and after a defiant sigh of resignation, he nodded. There would be other contests, other wins, and protesting with Raccs was not a good bet.

After retrieving his battle ax, Raccs sauntered over to the table and scooped up his two hundred credits. Then he gave a quizzical frown when he recognized a familiar face in the crowd smiling at him.

"Vinset? Is that you?"

Vinset nodded. "Quite the performance, my friend."

Raccs snorted. "Not much of one. The Baz'norean thought I did not know of his skill set. He believed he was maneuvering me when, in fact, I was maneuvering *him*." Raccs' simpleton demeanor vanished as he talked with Vinset. It also was part of the act.

"Still, well played." Vinset looked at the chips in

Raccs' massive hand. "So, how are your finances at the moment?"

The grin vanished from Raccs face. "In truth, not good. This is the most I have earned since I last saw you. It will pay for a meal and night's sleep, not much more."

"I understand." Vinset took Raccs by a massive arm and pulled him in a little closer. "I have a job for you … if you're in need of one."

"I am always in need of a job."

"Be warned: It doesn't pay much, maybe a thousand credits or so. But it will include lodging and meals for around forty days. There may even be some scavenging possible at the end."

"From the victims, of course?" Raccs asked, his grin returning.

"Of course. And there could be plenty to recover, such as weapons, credit satchels, items like that. Are you interested?"

"Let me consider for a moment: Scavenging, a thousand credits … and food and lodging for forty days? Yes, I am interested!"

Vinset grinned. *That makes three of them.* His recruitment efforts were off to a good start.

Vinset's next stop was at the administrative complex where he'd first seen The Human. It was at the magistrate's section, more precisely, the jail. As he was led to the holding section, Vinset wasn't surprised at what he found when he and the guard reached their destination.

It was a standard setup, with a set of five large chambers separated by blackened metal bars. Each cell had creatures in them, with two reserved exclusively for native Nefareans. These were drunk and/or obnoxious bulls who could prove deadly to other prisoners. One cell was exclusively for females, while the other two held an assortment of species. Overall, the scene was mostly peaceful, with the detainees respecting each other's privacy while waiting for a determination of their status, be it temporary or more permanent.

But the fifth cell was different. Sixteen prisoners, mostly of different species, were huddled against the left side of the enclosure, crowded next to each other, with three nursing cut wounds as best they could without professional care. None of their injuries were serious, just annoying. On the right side of the cell, only one creature was there, sitting on his haunches and bobbing slightly while licking two-inch-long claws, most with blood on them. Intense, unblinking yellow eyes were focused on the other prisoners ten feet away. It was obvious no one was going to infringe on the territory of the golden-haired, cat-like creature. Not again.

"Prisoner Jornay," the guard stated. "Your fine has been paid. You are free to go."

The cat creature didn't have to be told twice. He sprung from the seat and to the door in a single movement, retracting his claws so as not to startle the guard. As the door was unlocked and opened, Jornay took note of the other person with the guard.

"You are … Vinset." Then Jornay motioned with his hand outward as he extended his tongue. It was long—about six inches—but nowhere near as long as Vinset's. Still, the blond alien got the message.

"You are correct. How have you been, Jornay? It has been a couple of months."

"It has. I still have visions of the game we shared that night. I am fortunate I could not last as long as you."

"You did not have a starship to wager."

"Neither do you … now." Jornay looked back into the cell. "Are you replacing me as a guest of the Nefareans?"

"No, I am not; in fact, it was I who paid your fine to set you free." Vinset shook his head. "Seventy-five credits, and you could not pay that amount."

Jornay snickered, a high-pitched kind of squeal. "I did not have a starship to lose, but I did have everything else to lose, and I did. It has not been good for me since then. It was only food I stole, a necessity of life. I felt justified ... since it was either that or starve." Then Jornay frowned. "You paid my fine? Why? You do not owe me favors."

"I'm in need of your particular set of skills. There's a job for which you would be perfect."

"How much is the pay?"

Now it was Vinset's turn to frown. "Does it matter? It is more than you would earn in a holding cell. And now you do owe me a favor."

Jornay lifted his right hand, and instantly a set of five deadly claws shot out of the fingertips. "Does the job involve the use of these?" There was a wicked grin on Jornay's face. He glanced into the cell and watched the prisoners recoil.

"Very much so, along with your other skills."

"Then you are correct; it does not matter. Lead on, Vinset. I am anxious to make new friends ... as I have here."

10

After Jornay, Vinset's remaining circle of mercenary friends ended up being a bust. Either they weren't interested in working for such low wages, or they were gone or dead ... or both. The merc community was always in flux, with viable practitioners constantly moving, looking for new opportunities.

Adam returned from Calamont three days later with a cache of forty-eight MKs and six Xan-fis, having cost the miners an additional five thousand credits above the eight thousand for the hired guns. Adam apologized, telling Suma and the others that he was shocked by the price inflation affecting the weapons market. He had his own supply of guns provided by Tidus and Starfire Security, so rarely did he have to go out into the open market to buy them. But still, it would be enough. With the twenty-nine weapons they already had, forty-eight more MKs would give the miners seventy-seven, enough to arm the most physically fit males in the colony. Then between Adam, Vinset and the six used Xan-fis from Calamont, there were eleven long-barrel flash weapons available. It would have to do.

Adam was frustrated by this point, having already loaded one of his last two fuel pods into the gravity generator of the *Arieel* as he made the quick trip to Calamont and back. He was already in the hole on this job. And now he was going to loan out some of his—Starfire's—weapons inventory to what were not only strangers but amateurs. If they didn't get themselves killed using them, they would surely mess up the equipment. He regretted his decision to help, but it was too late by the time he returned from buying the guns. Vinset already had two more mercs, and preparations were underway for leaving Nefar. The wheels were in motion; it was too late for him to bail out now.

Adam, Vinset, Raccs and Jornay were aboard the *Arieel*, trying to decide if they could all fit inside for the twenty-hour flight to Sandicor. It would have been fine if Raccs wasn't so big. But fortunately, no one had to sleep. If they had to doze, they could do it in the common room. In addition, Adam could sleep at the pilot's station. Hell, he'd done that plenty of times in the past.

"Inside the starship, can you hear me?"

The airlock door was open, and Adam poked his head around a bulkhead corner to see who was outside. It was a near-featureless gray creature about seven feet tall and with long arms, easily three-quarters his height. Large black eyes blinked slowly, almost hypnotically.

"Yeah, what can I do for you?"

"I am Nanomin. There is word that you are seeking members for a mercenary team that will be heading out soon. Are you at capacity?"

There were only four mercs, and Adam considered that the bare minimum. Technically, they still had some of the eight thousand left, although, after Vinset's two thousand, the rest would be equally shared with the other team members. Even so, they'd discussed whether four would be enough. That would mean having to rely on the miners to pick up more of the fighting, something none of them were confident with.

"We could use another. What are your skills?"

"May I enter? It will require a demonstration."

The other mercs heard the conversation and were

as curious as Adam. They made room for Nanomin in the common room.

"I accept the role of traditional mercenary work, meaning I am proficient in a variety of weapons, including Xan-fi, Innis, MK and even a few Human varieties of ballistics. I am also skilled in all levels of electronics, including security systems, alarms, detonators and the sort."

"Okay, that sounds good," Adam said. "But without references, we can only take your word for it. And what was this demonstration you wanted to give?"

Nanomin moved in closer to Adam. "I also possess an ability mostly unique to my race, although I have heard of this on a variety of worlds but not to this degree. I shall give you proof—"

Nanomin reached out a long arm and wrapped his fingers around Adam's forearm....

Adam woke with a gaggle of alien faces looking down at him, not knowing how long he'd been out. The last thing he remembered was the gray alien grabbing his arm ... and then nothing. Although he was now on the deck, he didn't feel drugged or groggy. Still, Vinset and Jornay helped him to his feet and then guided him to the couch. Raccs was standing near the gray creature; an MK leveled at him.

"What happened?" Adam asked.

"He shocked you somehow," Vinset explained. "Sent you to the deck in a split second."

"I commend you, Human," Nanomin said. "It took more than I was expecting to subdue you."

"You shocked me? How?"

"My species generates a considerable electrical charge which we can channel through our bodies. I gave you only a small dose, just enough to get your attention. I apologize. I should have warned you—and the others—beforehand."

"You almost got yourself shot," Raccs growled.

"However, the demonstration was effective," Nanomin stated. "As I said, I have other skills, but it is my natural ability to deliver up to a killing shock that is the most unexpected. It has proved to be one of my most valuable assets." The grey alien grinned. "I can also short out nearly any electrical circuit I wish."

Adam looked at the faces of the other team members. As a group, they nodded.

"Well, Nano—sorry, I forgot your name."

"It is Nanomin, but everyone calls me Nanni."

"Okay, Nanni, welcome to the team. I hope you enjoy working for the bare minimum because that is all the job pays."

Nanni laughed. "It is more the ride off of Nefar that I need most. You see, I sometimes let my natural ability get the best of me, and there is an affluent

Nefarean undergoing medical care as we speak who would very much like to get his horns into me. I hope you understand."

They did—all of them.

And now there were five.

11

It had been decided that Raccs should ride with the miners aboard their ship back to Sandicor. It wasn't a long-range vessel, as was the *Arieel*, but it had more interior space. And with the addition of Nanni, Adam's ship was full.

It had been six days since Adam first met the miners, and a lot had happened in that time, including a whirlwind journey to Calamont and back. But now it was time to leave Nefar. The next flare event was only fourteen days away, and then Suma said Chanco would show up eight days later, once the stellar ejecta reached the planet, were collected and had time to be refined. If nothing else, the raider was predictable, which became the mercs' main advantage. They knew the time and place where he would next appear.

A rapping came on the metal hull of the *Arieel* just as Adam was making a final check of the focusing rings. Number two had been a little twitchy coming back from Calamont. He would take a closer look at it once he got back to Tel'oran.

Adam triggered the outer airlock door from the engine room and then made his way forward. Vinset and Jornay were waiting in the common room when a fit-looking young alien came into the ship and looked around with confidence and bravado.

The alien wore an expensive suit with velvet lapels and a vest made specifically for his race of six arms. A lot of species had six arms; after two arms, it was the most common, even more than four. Some of the species had arms that were all the same size, while some—including this one—had four fully formed arms and then two smaller ones that were used exclusively to funnel food into the lower stomach. This particular configuration included what was called *min* and *nin* arms in certain cultures, but Adam couldn't remember which were which, the upper or the lower. It didn't matter. But what it did was make for an interesting cut of his garment to accommodate all his weird appendages.

And this alien was weirder than most. He carried on him four sets of holsters, each made of polished plastic and fitted perfectly to the K-90s he wore. The K-90 was MK's latest—and most expensive—handgun. It had nearly double the capacity of an '88, including a targeting computer that was near instantaneous. A few years back, Xan-fi flirted with linking to a shooter's brain for targeting, syncing with their eyesight. That hadn't gone over too well when it was learned that the Milky Way Klin were using the subcutaneous linking chips to control the brains of the subjects. Since then, the weapons manufacturers had returned to traditional targeting through radar-like computers, working to speed up the locking times rather than through neural links. The '90 was the top of the line in that regard.

Adam scanned the young dandy from top to bottom, estimating that he probably had five thousand EUs worth of weaponry on him, shaming the amount Adam had just spent on used MK-17s.

"What's your business here?" Adam asked, already sensing why the alien was there.

"I understand you are looking for hired guns. I am here to offer my services. I am a warrior."

Adam looked at Vinset, who frowned and cocked his head. Then turning his attention back to the newcomer, Adam said, "You're kinda young for this line of work, aren't you? What's your name?"

"I am Flinn, and age is not important. Skill is what counts in a profession such as this."

Adam stepped closer. "Then I'd say that by the look of your clothes and your equipment, you must be extremely skilled, enough to demand the highest fees. Either that or you come from wealth. Which is it?"

"My wealth has nothing to do with my skill," the alien said defensively, which answered Adam's question. "I am unique in that I am proficient with *all* my weapons, which, as I can see, is many more than the rest of you can carry."

Adam pursed his lips and nodded. "That is true; you have four guns where we only have one each. But do you draw and fire all four at the same time? If so, how do you do that? Do you have a set of eyes for each weapon and four brains to process the targets? It seems to me this is overkill. I would get the same effect if I carried one weapon and then had three backups. Is that how it is with you?"

For an answer, Flinn pulled his four MKs simultaneously, aiming two to the left and two to the right. Adam was surprised he had the coordination to do so. But he also noticed none of the draws were particularly fast.

Nanni moved a little closer to Flinn, ready to shock him if need be. Adam shook his head, indicating he could handle this.

Adam nodded to the young alien. "That's very good. But how often are you facing four shooters at a time? And if you were, then you would have to worry not about all four but only about the individual who is faster than you. And it only takes one to kill you."

"I am faster than—"

That was as far as he got before Adam had his MK-88 out and pressed against Flinn's smooth-skinned forehead. The alien stared crossed-eyed at the barrel of the weapon, holding his breath.

Adam smiled and holstered the gun.

"Let's try that again. You draw your *four* weapons before I can draw mine. I want to see if there's strength in numbers, as you seem to believe. You go whenever you're ready."

The young alien reholstered his armada and stood facing Adam, his four arms spaced apart and only inches from the pistol grips. He hesitated.

"Whenever you want."

Flinn jumped when Adam spoke. And then he took a deep breath.

Adam watched the eyes. At the moment of action, they would widen ever so slightly; Adam didn't even have to watch the hands to know when.

And then it came, the widening.

Adam had his weapon out and up in a blur and once again pressed against the alien's forehead, even before the first of Flinn's four barrels cleared their holsters.

Adam knew it wasn't a fair contest; no one in the room could match Adam at draw speed, not even

Jornay with his cat-like reflexes. But it was a good lesson for the kid to learn. Numbers weren't everything. Adam only needed one gun to kill him.

Flinn released his weapons and glared at Adam.

"Speed is not the only measure. Accuracy counts as well."

"True, but I don't need accuracy with the barrel pressed against your head."

"Why are you doing this to me?" the alien screeched. "I have come here to help, to be part of this adventure. I do not even need the fee. And I have my own ship."

"This isn't an adventure, my friend," Vinset said. "This is serious work. We are risking our lives and need our companions to cover our flanks in battle. Have you ever been in combat?"

"I … I know all about combat."

"From the Library?" Jornay queried.

Flinn scanned the faces in the room. None were mocking him, but all were serious. They were saving his life, even if he didn't know it.

Flinn's jaw locked, and his eyes burned into Adam.

"I have heard the stories about the *great* Human, killer of thousands, conquer of worlds. No fugitive is safe when he is on the trail. But not only that, but he is the supreme tactician, leading battles on a dozen worlds without a single loss. And when I learned you were assembling a force for yet another great adventure, I wanted to be part of it."

"Why?" Adam asked.

"To work with you, to learn from you."

"Is your life so shallow that you can afford to lose it at such a young age?" Adam asked. "No, Flinn. Go home, go back to your family. I'm sure they're worried about you and this strange quest you're on to *find* yourself." Adam waved a hand at the others in the rooms. "We are all desperate individuals, doing what we have to do to make a living. We don't do this because we enjoy it or out of a sense of adventure. We do it because it's the only life we know. I'm sure your family has a better life ready for you. Accept it. And then live long … and prosper." Adam fought back a laugh from his last sentence, along with the urge to raise his hand in a Vulcan salute. None of the aliens in the room would understand the context.

"You know nothing of my family and what it is like to grow up as one of thirty offspring. We all must work to stand out in some way. I have sought a life of adventure, protecting the innocent, with a purpose for my living."

"You're not a superhero," Adam pointed out. "You're just confused."

"And getting yourself killed on some faraway rock will not make you stand out," Vinset added. "At least not in any meaningful way. Take Adam's advice. Go home … and live."

Flinn's eyes were watery, and his lips trembled. "I have had enough of you—all of you—you losers. I accept what you say about your pitiful lives. You are desperate; I can see it in your eyes. But *my* life has meaning. I *will* count for something."

And with that, Flinn stormed out of the *Arieel*.

"Crazy, mixed-up kid," Adam said, quoting a line from an old Western movie he'd seen years ago. Then he shrugged and looked at his watch. "I hope we don't have any more surprise guests before we leave. Suma and the others are lifting off in an hour. Let's button things up. Our so-called *adventure* is about to begin."

12

The journey to Sandicor was uneventful, but that changed when Adam took the *Arieel* down for a low sweep over the planet to get a lay of the land.

First of all, the planet was small, about half the size of Earth, which meant the gravity would be much lower. But size wasn't the only determinant of gravity. Density also matters. Adam studied the meters, which could determine surface gravity by measuring the fractional differences at various elevations and then extrapolating the changes to the ground. Sandicor would be about four-point-eight-tenths that of Adam's homeworld, and that would definitely give him a strength advantage in the coming battle.

Adam snorted, trying not to draw attention to himself as the cockpit was crowded with the other three team members who made the short trip with him from Nefar. They were looking out the forward viewport, not as tourists, but as warriors, studying the terrain should any of them have to venture outside.

He'd snorted because Adam had a secret. Besides Humans' natural strength advantage over most aliens, Adam had a few extra tricks up his sleeve. First, he always kept the internal gravity of the *Arieel* set at a quarter higher than Earth standard, at least when he wasn't transporting alien passengers. This conditioned his body, helping to make up for the loss of bone and muscle mass he suffered while on alien worlds with lower gravity. And second, was his continual cloning. Although incredibly slow acting, the process helped keep his muscles and other bodily systems in top-notch condition. He wouldn't be allowed to age until he reached the end of the cloning. When would that be? Not even the mutant geniuses who performed the cloning knew the answer. It may not be until he reached his last non-cloned age of fifty-six. And even then, it could take a hundred years to reach that point, at which time he would start to age normally. Honestly, Adam had no idea how long he would live before he died of natural causes. However, it was the unnatural causes that would probably get him. And Adam Cain seemed determined to test that proposition seemingly every day of his extended life.

But for now, Adam would land on the planet

Sandicor with a distinct advantage. His Earth weight of one hundred eighty pounds would be more like ninety here, and his overly conditioned muscles would probably reduce that by another ten to twenty. And that's why he snickered. On Sandicor, *The Human* would be a god-damn superman—or *superalien*—as he'd begun to call himself. On Earth, he'd still fall within the range of the top weightlifters and normal Humans. But this was outer space, and Adam would take all the advantages he could get.

He now shifted his attention to the surface of Sandicor. They were on the dark side, the perpetual night of the planet, where the temperature hovered around two-hundred degrees below zero Fahrenheit. It didn't reach the near absolute cold of space because of the thin atmosphere that constantly swirled at over a hundred miles per hour. It would be heated on one side and then sweep around to the other, cooling before swinging back around again.

But still, there were massive glaciers that filled nearly every deep valley, along with towering peaks approaching forty-thousand feet in height. And then the closer one got to the terminal zone—the transition between night and day—the moisture in the atmosphere would condense and fall in constant downpours, feeding short-lived streams and rivers. They flowed toward the light, at which time the water would boil and evaporate, to be sucked up into the atmosphere again to make another trip around the planet.

All this geologic and climatic action made for a colorful and dynamic landscape as the *Arieel* came up on the transition zone. Some called this region the *Twilight Zone*, and they weren't wrong, either scientifically or in Adam's context, as an area of strange happenings.

"Take us to the starside," Vinset said. "That's where the collectors are located."

Adam obliged, and before they landed at the miner's settlement, he piloted the starship into the blazing light of the nearby star. Everyone aboard had seen stars up close and planets with boiling landscapes even closer to their parent star than Sandicor was to Minos. Even so, the scene was hellish and frightening. Why anyone would choose to settle on a world like this was unfathomable.

And then they came upon the collector array.

They stood out from the scorched black rocks by their steel grey surfaces that reflected the brilliance of Minos. They were stationary structures since the surface orientation to the star hadn't changed in a billion years. In Adam's opinion, they were shaped like giant Doritos and held to the surface by dozens of thick cables anchored into the crusty ground. Their surface was made of a grid of wires and panels designed to capture the incoming ejecta from the coronal mass eruptions and then filter it through the system until it reached equipment rooms under the collectors. According to Suma, most of the process of filtering for Element-129 was done automatically by the collectors. But the last step was to remove the concentrate and refine it even further within the underground colony. Since the material is radioactive, this required shielding, special equipment and specific training. Suma and Forlin were being trained as refiners while Rilos worked in the crews that maintained the underworld community.

After a brief foray into Hell, Adam returned the *Arieel* to the more temperate Twilight Zone, linking up with Suma's ship to be guided to the landing areas. Along the way, Suma got on the comm and gave the team a running narration, describing what they saw below.

"We are approaching the three Peace Palaces—as we call them." On the surface were a trio of clear domes with what looked to be gardens and greenbelts growing inside. There were people in the domes, and they stopped and looked up as the pair of ships made their pass. "Life underground would be intolerable if it weren't for the chance to visit the domes for a walk within nature or to gaze up at the stars. The Palaces are placed closer to the dark side to afford this opportunity. We also capture river water for irrigation and recreation before most of it is recycled on the starside."

The ships slowed and began to hover above a large metal plate on the ground. "The community consists of over ninety miles of underground tunnels, with more being worked on all the time," Suma continued. "As such, there are numerous entrances to the city, including the official six landing bays. However, only two are designed to handle ships as large as ours. The others are reserved for small planetary hoppers or orbital vessels, most left over from the time when the colony was being built. We will land below and then be lowered underground where the chamber will be atmosphered. Because we can place environment locks at the end of any surface tunnel, we have dozens, including access hatches near the collectors."

"That's a lot of ways in and out," Vinset commented.

"I was thinking the same thing," Adam said. "We're going to have to close off a lot of those," he said to Suma.

"Why? Chanco only comes in through the largest landing ports."

"That's good to know. But we're concerned about ways he can escape once the shooting starts."

"Ah," Suma said. "You are already planning the event."

Adam snickered. "We're not on vacation, Suma. We've come to do a job."

"I respect that immensely. Now follow me to the surface. The landing procedure is straightforward."

Once underground, Adam was awestruck by the size of the cavern they were in. Suma noticed him gawking as they met up in the still frigid air that had just filled the chamber.

"Come, I will take you to our leader, Tansin," Suma said. "He is very anxious to hear of your plan. And along the way, I will tell you the story of my home."

The miner was bursting with pride, something Adam found incongruous. Who could be proud of living like a groundhog?

"In the past, Sandicor was highly volcanic, the result of a wildly elliptical orbit that deformed the planet constantly," Suma said, beginning the tour. Adam noticed the uniform red of the rock, resembling hardened lava. "Then, as the orbit stabilized to what it is now, the vulcanism ceased, leaving behind enormous caverns, lava tubes and other formations. Then over the three hundred years we have been here, the colonists have carved out larger chambers."

They'd left the landing chamber and were now in a tunnel easily fifty yards wide and disappearing around gradual turns. Adam rubbed a hand across the surface. It was smooth, as if polished. Suma noticed.

"Yes, we shape the walls. The material is easy to work, and we have the equipment. It is a matter of pride for us that our settlement be clean and designed. There are natural chambers and tunnels—such as the landing area—but most of the living area is like this. Let me give you an example."

Suma moved up to a doorway set along the tunnel wall. There were electronics attached to the smoothed rock. He pressed a button, and a moment later, a red-skinned female opened the door. She didn't appear surprised to see Suma and the other aliens.

"I have been watching the arrival on the broadcast," she said to Suma. Then she looked to Adam. "I am honored to meet the others who have come to help. Would you care to tour my home?"

Adam got the sense this visit was pre-arranged, a way to introduce the mercenaries to how the miners lived. They stepped through the door and into an impressive chamber easily a hundred feet across and towering half that high. A half dozen doorways or tunnels led off from the circular living room, telling Adam that what he saw was only a fraction of the home's true size.

"There are only three hundred of us in the colony," Suma explained. "As such, there is no shortage of space for each abode. If a family unit or individual wishes a home, as a community, we help carve out the chamber for the occupant or occupants. We are generous with our time and effort. Most of our homes are of comparable size to this one. Again, we feel it helps us cope with what we are missing by not living on a more traditional world. I live single, yet my abode is approximately the size of this one." He grinned. "However, the large size does require extra time to clean."

They didn't look in all the rooms, but the tour was impressive. Although he knew they were underground, Adam didn't feel claustrophobic. Everything was oversize in the colony, and now he knew it was by design.

"Do you have a name for your colony," Nanni asked Suma.

He laughed. "Since its inception, there has been talk of naming the colony. But since it is the only settlement on Sandicor, we have always called it that. I realize this can be confusing. Just know that Sandicor and the colony are one and the same."

They left the home and continued along the main concourse. More miners and their families were coming out to see the strangers, although none appeared frightened; in fact, a few looked hostile, glaring at Adam and crew with unblinking alien eyes. Adam would reserve judgment. These might be the more forward-thinking members of the colony, those who realized what was about to happen. To Adam,

Sandicor—meaning the colony—had crossed the Rubicon. There was no turning back, not if they wanted things to change. And, according to Suma, if things didn't change, their days were numbered.

Adam scanned the faces of his team, glad to see that there were no tourists among them. Each was looking up and down and all around—as was he—checking for cover locations, ingress and egress points, along with ambush spots. Chanco had over forty raiders. From past experience, Adam knew that confined areas, such as the tunnels, negated numerical superiority … if the ground could be held. He'd personally seen hundreds of attackers fall to a small but determined defensive unit. It all depended on how willing the attackers were to die. And raiders may be tough and pragmatic, but they weren't fanatics; they were in it for the money and what it could buy. And dead aliens couldn't buy much … only their funerals.

Suma brought them to a large double-door entry and pushed it open. It spread apart on balanced hinges to reveal a carved-out shell-shaped room with a raised presentation stage to the left and rows of elevated seating climbing to the right. There were a few natives in the room, mainly on the stage. Adam had decided to call the miners natives in his mind, although they weren't indigenous to Sandicor. But they were the only game in town.

A tall, older alien with yellow skin perked up when

Suma entered with the mercs. Adam was putting on his game face. He was sure a presentation had to be made to the leader with him explaining how Adam expected the defensive of Sandicor to go down. As always in situations like these, he debated whether to lay it on thick and honest or temper it a little so as to not scare the children. Either way, at this point in an operation, no one wanted to hear the truth.

"If it pleases you," Suma said to Adam and the others, "I wish to present to you Tansin Eso, the current elected leader of Sandicor. Tansin, this is the being known as *The Human*, along with his team of experienced mercenary soldiers who have come to help defend our colony against Chanco and his bandits. With your indulgence, the Human will detail the plan he has devised."

The creature bowed slightly and looked confused.

"Greetings," Tansin said, "Although it is a pleasure to meet you, your emissary has already introduced you and detailed the plan. I must say, it is quite impressive, especially for such a small force."

Adam frowned. "Emissary? What emissary."

"Your emissary." Tansin looked to the upper rows of seating, to a figure in a shiny blue jacket with velvet lapels. "There he is … Flinn; I believe he said his name is."

The six-armed dandy stood, stretching four of them wide as he grinned at Adam.

"Yes, welcome, my friends," Flinn said, his voice carrying easily across the room, as it was designed to do. "Having arrived four hours early in my speeder, I have been informing Tansin and the other colonists of the heroic gesture we are about to embark upon on their behalf. They are quite enamored with the prospect."

"Did you tell them they will be required to join in the effort," Adam asked, his jaw firm, his eyes glaring.

"I did, indeed. And according to Tansin, most are enthusiastic about the prospect."

"Most?"

"The others will acquiesce as their training progresses. I have begun organizing the assessment process so as to best determine who is to fill critical missions. I have even begun distributing weapons."

"What weapons?" Suma asked. He had never seen Flinn before and was confused that he claimed to be part of the mercenary team. He looked at Adam and whispered, "He is a sixth member of your team? I did not know. How will we pay him?"

The question carried across the acoustically designed room. "As I explained to Elder Tansin, I come free," Flinn answered.

"Is that so?" Suma asked Adam.

"Apparently."

"Kac-Flinn has been quite enthusiastic about the mission," Tansin remarked. "Some of that energy is now filtering throughout Sandicor, energy which is sorely needed as nerves have been frayed by the uncertainty of the coming ordeal. And the weapons—magnificent weapons—also a gift. We are glad to have kac-Flinn and the others here to help us."

Adam pursed his lips, upset that Flinn had pressed his hand but glad to have extra guns and someone to wield them, even if that someone could be more bombast than skill. But he was here now; whatever happened to him after this was of his own making.

Adam waved for Flinn to join the others on the stage. The young alien happily obliged. He moved proudly up beside Adam, grinning widely while looking at Tansin and the other natives.

Adam leaned over and whispered, "Slick move, asshole. Let's just hope this doesn't come back to bite us in the ass."

Flinn listened for a moment with the grin still on his face. Then it slowly dissolved, and the alien looked over at Adam with a frown. "I heard the words and the translation; however, I have no concept of what you just said."

"You'll figure it out ... if you live long enough."

Adam now took a look at his ragtag group of mercenaries; six strange creatures, each of different species.

He hadn't seen such an oddball collection of beings in a while, and they were all under his command. He recalled a quote he'd read, attributed to the author J. Clifton Slater: *'The unaffiliated driftwood of ruined civilizations washed ashore to foul the atmosphere of a foreign land.'* Adam snorted. You could say that again. They definitely weren't *The A-Team*. Hell, they weren't even *The Magnificent Seven*. But they certainly were *The Assorted Six*.

13

Finding it redundant and possibly contradictory at this point to detail the plan—as tentative as it was—to Tansin, Adam and his people were shown to a *building* that resembled a hotel. As with all the others, it was carved out of the rock and consisted of several huge rooms, all of which were larger than any hotel rooms Adam had ever seen, complete with grooming stations, food processors, a sleeping area and a living room. A massive monitor was on the wall displaying a pastoral scene obviously from some other planet. It was made to look like a picture window when in reality, it was a recording.

Adam found it confusing—and a little sad—that people who lived underground, and had done so for three hundred years, would work so hard to trick themselves into believing it wasn't so bad. It had to be the price they paid for living on a hell world. Normally, just about any Prime world had a variety of environments, something suitable for everyone. But not so on Sandicor. There was no suitable environment on the surface of the planet that forced the natives to cheat reality rather than accept it. After three hundred years, it must be working; otherwise, they would have abandoned the facility centuries ago.

Once settled into his room, Adam pulled a datapad from his satchel and scanned his battle notes. They were a series of concerns, questions and ideas about how to deal with the complexities of the mission. Although this assignment had a few more moving parts than did his other mercenary jobs, they were all about the same. He had to consider the environment, personnel, supplies, the opposing force and the timing, among other things. Once these topics were evaluated, only then could he design a strategy that took each subject into consideration.

Also, in each operation, there was a main advantage and disadvantage to be considered, along with other minor concerns. The main advantage of this operation was the element of surprise. But that would only last for a few minutes. During this time, Adam and his team had to inflict maximum damage on the enemy before they had a chance to regroup and reorganize.

The disadvantage was the size of the opposition in

relation to the force he could bring against it ... among other things. He hadn't yet reached the point where he could count the natives as an asset. And if they weren't an asset, were they a liability? Would they get in the way more than help? And would he and his people react differently to protect innocents against friendly fire and collateral damage rather than deliver full force to the enemy and let the civilians be damned? Since they filled the role of the good guys in every battle, Adam's side always had to take that into consideration. Not so Chanco. The bad guys didn't give a damn about who they hurt.

A secondary advantage was the terrain. If Adam could control where the raiders entered the complex and how they would leave, he could create a deadly gauntlet that would cut the opposing force down to size. For that, he would have to survey the layout of the colony closely while also learning of Chanco's habits from the other times he'd come. Was he consistent, or did he change his routine? Was he careless or cautious? And if Adam made too many changes in order to route the raiders within the tunnels, would he notice?

There was a myriad of questions that had to be answered before Adam drew up a final battle plan. That was what concerned him. What had Flinn already told the natives about the attack? And where did he get his information?

Adam huffed. *He made it up; that's where,* he thought.

And made it up from his years of training and experience in the art of war. Even in his mind, the sarcasm was ripe.

Now Adam cringed. He had to talk with the young alien just to keep their stories straight while at the same time learning how much damage control he had to do to set things right.

Flinn was a few doors down the hall, which from the size of the rooms, was about three hundred feet away. As Adam stepped out of his room, he felt the fresh breeze of circulated air. The natives had to import everything to keep their colony alive, even air, and they had done a remarkable job of it. For being on such a harsh world, they did a pretty good job of making it comfortable, even pleasant.

Flinn was in his room, with his four K-90s on a table as he cleaned them. One of the weapons was in pieces, and the alien made a special effort to show Adam how fast he could reassemble the gun. *Not bad*, Adam thought, *for someone's hobby.* But then he wondered if Flinn had ever fired the weapons in anger or need. Had he ever killed anyone?

So he asked.

"You ridicule me without knowledge," the alien chided. "For three standard years, I have been accepting assignments where my skill with a weapon was required, and I am still alive. Yes, I have fired at an enemy; I even have verified kills. Does that settle your doubt?"

"Did you kill up close? And have you ever had to fight for your life without a weapon?"

"A complex question requiring a complex answer. For the first part, yes, I have killed an opponent as close to me as you are. As far as the second part, no, I have not been required to physically fight another creature, although I have been trained in physical combat. As you have surmised, my family has wealth, and as a consequence, I have been afforded the most advanced and expert training my wealth can purchase. In your opinion, that may not qualify, but short of initiating a fight within a tavern, I know not how I can gain such experience without engaging in actual and unscripted combat. That is what I seek, the experience you value so much. But how does one gain such experience without seeking it out in whatever manner is available? You, Human, obviously have military training attained on your homeworld. That was not an option for me. And that is why I seek it in other ways, through you and the others."

Adam had to give the kid credit; he was determined. He was also right. Adam grew up in the military; his father was a Navy Master Chief. He had always considered the military as his only career path. That had led to a brief career as a Navy SEAL, brief because after only seven years in the service, he was abducted by aliens, those aliens being the evil Klin. So, how much could he criticize the young alien? Flinn was born into a world of wealth and privilege, but maybe that wasn't the life he saw for himself. Maybe he didn't want to live a pre-programmed life. Maybe he wanted to be … Adam Cain.

"Okay, kid, I'll cut you some slack—"

"Please, speak more clearly! How do the others understand you? How do they follow your commands when you constantly speak in Human code?"

Adam laughed. There was something about Flinn that made Adam throw away his normal way of interacting with aliens and become more casual, more … fatherly? Was that it? Did Adam feel a paternal connection to the young alien, seeing him as the son he never had? Adam had two daughters; one now deceased, the other immortal—that was a dichotomy he'd never actually realized before. It was strange how the universe balanced the books. But now he'd apparently taken a young male under his wing and was doing all he could to protect him. Why? And especially now. Comparing the two, they didn't look much different in age, although Flinn had to be in his late teens from the look of it, while Adam was in his early twenties and would be for years to come.

That revelation settled a lot of things in his head.

"Very well, Flinn. You're now an official member

of my team. I appreciate your help and dedication to the cause. I just want to make sure you understand what the cause truly is and not get lost in some fantasy version of what we do."

"To protect the colony against Chanco at all costs, that is our mission."

Adam smirked and shook his head. "Yeah, that's the official purpose. But in our line of work, the number one goal is to come home alive." Adam saw the shocked look on Flinn's face. "Is that surprising to you?"

"What is surprising is that *you* would say it. You are the famous *Human*. You are constantly risking your life for others."

"It's a measured risk. Also, most of my jobs have to do with organizing attacks and defenses and not actually fighting in them. One person usually doesn't make a difference between success and failure, so I try to stay out of the fighting as much as possible. I'm like the general conducting the battlefield rather than the soldier in the trenches."

"I understand that from your point of view."

"And another thing. I have a certain skill set that I know like the back of my hand … that I know really well. I also know that this is not our fight. No contract work ever is. However, we make it our fight, but within limitations. After all, we're supposed to be the brains of the operation and not the foot soldiers. We'll fight, but only up to the point where winning is no longer a possibility. After that, all bets are off, meaning it's time to cut bait … I mean, it's time to leave. Sacrificing ourselves for a cause that is not our own is simply a waste of life."

"Do you have this cynical attitude with every assignment you take?"

Adam shrugged. "Pretty much. I've been accused of having a bad attitude before, and in most cases, it's true. Let me explain it this way. We have a saying on my world that says we need to have *skin in the game* to make it count. That means there has to be something of value at stake, and I don't mean a payday at the end. I mean something that's important to you—vital—like your life or the lives of people you care for. It can also be to protect your country—or world—as it is with military personnel. Or from a deep feeling of responsibility to a creed or oath, such as with law enforcement."

"I must say, I am shocked at the revelation you have bestowed on me. Is this the attitude of other mercenaries you have worked with?"

"Yeah, at least the ones still alive. There have been others who became too involved in their mission that they forgot about rule number one."

"To come home alive?"

"To come home alive."

Adam could still see the young warrior-wannabe

wasn't convinced.

"Don't get me wrong. Sometimes during a mission, you can become part of the struggle, so much so that it becomes the *skin* you have in the game. It becomes your mission, along with those who hired you. That's fine, too. But you can't treat *every* mission that way; otherwise, there won't be too many missions on your resume."

"Resume?"

"Never mind. Let's just say your missions will be limited. You can't be willing to die for every job; it's as simple as that."

"I see the logic in your argument; I just did not realize logic was such an important variable."

Adam recoiled. "You didn't? What do you think drives us as mercenaries?"

"Adventure."

Adam laughed. "Are we back on that again? No, adventure is not what drives us. It's logic as we weigh each mission, determining our chances of coming out of it alive. Doesn't that make more sense? If the odds are against you surviving, then you don't take the job."

"And you believe we can defeat Chanco?"

"I do, but again, it may not be your definition of *defeat*. I think we can hurt him enough so that he will never return, or it will take him a while to recover. But as far as total defeat goes—of us killing every last one of his bandits—I think that's a little unrealistic. I'm here to help because I'm pissed at Chanco and his raiders. But that anger will only go so far. I have enough confidence in my abilities—and luck—that I'm pretty sure I'll make it out alive. It's you I have my doubts about."

Flinn was silent for a moment until Adam broke it for him.

"But this isn't why I came here, to have a philosophical debate about being a mercenary. I came to find out what you told Tansin about the battle plan. What did you tell him?"

Flinn perked up. "I told him six of the mightiest warriors the galaxy had ever seen were coming to defend their colony. I told him we were dedicated to their safety and preservation and that we would not rest until the Chanco threat is eliminated completely." He stopped and frowned. "I see now that I must amend my statement, and in a number of ways."

"You can't do that, at least not now," Adam said with reluctance. "Contrary to your belief that the six of us can defeat Chanco on our own, we need the natives to help, if only to clutter up the battlefield with a bunch of random flash bolts from their out-of-date weapons."

"The weapons I gave them are not out-of-date."

"I mean the ones *I* got for them."

Flinn smirked and shrugged, which said all he had to.

14

The clock was ticking. It was six days until the next coronal mass ejection, and already the star Minos was acting up, sending pre-eruption spurts into space. These smaller events carried E-129 with them as well, just not very much. Conditions on the starside of Sandicor were heating up even more than normal.

While Jornay, Raccs, Nanni and Flinn began the screening process for fighters and arranged for a shooting range in one of the big caverns, Adam and Vinset accompanied Suma on a more detailed tour of the facility. They took one of the electric carts because they had a lot of territory to cover.

"Does Chanco always come in at the same landing pad?" Adam asked.

"He has, from what I recall," Suma answered. "I will check if there are records confirming this."

"And his troops, do they stay with him or fan out?" It was Vinset's turn to ask a question.

"His core soldiers remain with him. That can be anywhere from five to ten individuals. The others spread out, searching the abodes for valuables, either new or ones they may have missed during their prior visits. There is not much left; they are beginning to take personal mementos and the like, which is causing elevated consternation."

"Do they ever take the carts, or do they walk?"

"They walk."

"And they meet at the Grand Hall?"

"Usually, at first. Chanco may want to go to Tansin's office and partake in a beverage from the processor."

"And how long do they stay?" Adam asked.

"Not longer than a few hours. We are beginning to prepare the E-129 in small containers divided into ten-unit segments. It makes it easier for him to take his share and leave us the rest. The containers are shielded against the radiation. That way, he will leave sooner and take his thieving horde with him."

"And then they leave the same way, down the same passageways?" Vinset asked. "This passageway?"

Suma nodded.

"Okay," Adam began. "This way only takes him

about five minutes at the most to walk from the landing bay to the Grand Hall. We need them to take more time, a more convoluted path."

"Why is that?" Suma asked.

"I want to disorient them and for it to take longer for them to leave."

"Leave, not arrive?"

"We'll hit them initially at the Grand Hall," Adam explained. "But then they will run for the exits. We need to make sure they run the right way while giving us time to cut them down."

Adam looked at the ceiling. "Do you ever get cave-ins?"

Suma snorted. "All the time, especially during events. The magnetic field of Minos is disrupted, and that causes tremors on Sandicor."

"Good. We'll need your people to create some fake cave-ins. Gouge out the ceiling some and then place huge piles of debris in the tunnels, causing Chanco to take a different path. The debris will also give us positions to fire from. All the workers cleaning the piles should also be your best with weapons. Once Chanco and his soldiers pass, they'll take up positions and start firing. And, Suma, these cave-in locations need to be near long, open hallways with no side rooms. We want the bandits to have no place to hide."

Suma's eyes were wide with excitement. "That

sounds like an excellent plan. But what about the others, the bandits who are spread among the colony?"

"That could be a problem," Vinset said. "That is why there should be extensive cave-ins at a number of locations. The raiders shouldn't be allowed to spread out as normal. They need to go only where we want them to. They must be contained."

"Also," Adam said, "since there are more of us than there are of them, we should assign a squad of your people to each bandit as they move about the tunnels. Nothing overt, just so when the shooting starts, we have eyes on all of them. And portable communicators, do you have them?"

"We have enough. In addition, there is an excellent linking system within the colony for more static communications."

Adam nodded. They had come to the end of the tunnel, and Suma got out of the cart. "I wish to show you an outside access hatch. As I mentioned, there are many in Sandicor. You will find this interesting."

Adam and Vinset stepped through an opening secured by a heavy pressure door. Inside the smaller tunnel was a long series of steps carved out of the rock and leading up. It took almost ten minutes to reach the top.

"The living tunnels are intentionally deep on the starside because the heat tends to be absorbed far underground."

Adam felt the temperature increase the higher on the steps he climbed until it was almost unbearably hot at the top landing. There was an airlock at the top. The trio stepped inside. Suma allowed Adam and Vinset to move to the heavily polarized view window in the outer hatch.

What Adam saw was his vision of Hell. There was a yellow cast to the landscape, reflecting the blazing star in the sky. The surface looked flaky, with huge slabs of shiny black rock stacked on top of each other and at odd angles. Other mounds looked to be the remains of bubbling magma that spewed forth and then hardened, turning black in the process. And then there was the constant haze in the air from the windblown regolith, traveling at such velocity that it could sandblast just about any material down to atoms in a matter of hours. And it never let up, blowing from west to east, from the starside to the night side, driven by radical pressure swings around the globe.

Through the hazy wind, Adam could see one of the huge collectors. He was awed by the fact that it could weather the conditions outside, a marvel of modern alien technology. And then he thought of the cost of maintaining the colony and the mining equipment. It had to be astronomical, meaning the price for E-129—the colony's only cash crop—must be equally astronomical. What could the natives do with that money if Chanco didn't take it from them?

Even through the darkened glass, the scene was blinding.

"You go out into that?" Adam asked incredulously.

"As little as possible and only when necessary," Suma answered solemnly. "I lost a very good friend the last time I was outside. It was during the last harvest. It is a horrible way to die."

Then Suma led them back to the stairs.

"I wanted to show you that so you will know that using these access ports as escape routes for the raiders will be virtually impossible. It takes highly specialized suits to survive beyond this point, and there are only twelve of them in the entire colony. And even if one was to go outside in one, they could only remain for an hour under normal conditions, and half that time for several days following an event. And even in a suit, no one can survive the initial radiation blast from a coronal event. They strike Sandicor only minutes after an eruption."

"That's good to know; it's one less thing to worry about," Adam said. "If Chanco wants to go out in that, he's more than welcome."

The rest of the day was spent getting down to brass tacks. Adam and Vinset were provided with detailed schematics of the colony, and Suma helped pinpoint bottlenecks and covering positions where debris barriers could be set up. And then the natives got down to work. At first, they weren't too happy about it. They had spent so much time and energy making their passageways as pristine as possible, only to now be asked to clutter them with red rock and dust. And they weren't allowed to clean up any of the dust. It had to look as if the cave-ins had just occurred.

In the meantime, Flinn and his group had about a hundred of the younger, more fit natives in an echoing cavern with targets set up fifty feet away from a makeshift firing line. After Jornay gave a brief lesson on the basic functioning of the Maris-Kliss handguns, ten colonists at a time were moved up to the line and handed MKs.

At first, they were told to fire using the targeting computers so they could get a sense of how long the computer took to lock on and to sense the slight vibration in the grip when it was time to shoot. The problem with using the computers in combat was that the bandits would be running at full speed as the computers tried to lock on. And that wasn't going to happen. Even if a lock occurred, the moment the shooter moved the gun, the lock would be broken. And the natives had nervous hands. That was obvious.

After firing a couple of bolts at Level-2, the natives were then told to sight their targets and shoot for real this time, after which the qualifying bolts began to fly, lighting up the room. And fly they did. A target at fifty feet is a difficult distance for an old MK-17 to hit, even with a steady hand and strong lock on a stationary target. As a result, only two out of every ten shots even grazed the targets. And this went for the entire group of one hundred natives as they had their turn at the firing line.

Then they were told to turn off the computers and just sight and fire. Surprisingly, the success rate jumped to three out of ten. The best shooters in both categories were noted, and in the end, there were seventeen finalists who would be given premier spots within the tunnels and with the best weapons, including the Xanfi rifles. Most of the others were still issued weapons, and thanks to Flinn's contribution, there were enough to go around. This second tier of natives would be assigned posts, but not much would be expected of them. They would be used mainly for herding purposes, to direct Chanco and his thugs into the true killing fields.

So, with time and cooperation, a plan was coming together, and Adam was gaining confidence with each passing hour. But the proof would be in the pudding. And that would be when the shooting starts.

For the most part, the natives were pulling their weight, although there were still grumbles with awkward questions about what happens after the fighting stops. Adam had an answer, but the natives wouldn't like it, so he would save it for another day. For the time being, he wanted the miners focused on one event at a time, although for the natives, that event wasn't the arrival of Chanco and his bandits. To them, it was what was about to happen on the rumbling cauldron of incredible heat and energy that dominated the sky. Minos was getting ready to erupt, and Adam and his team were even more anxious than the natives to see a coronal mass eruption up close and personal. To the natives, this was old hat. To Adam and the others, it was an *adventure*.

15

As the time for the eruption neared, Flinn found himself in the collection control room with Nanni, surveying the ancient equipment while shaking his head and wondering how the natives were able to salvage anything from the collectors. He went from post to post, snorting and huffing, checking model numbers of the units and then snorting and huffing some more.

Diyanna Ganz was at her station, one that was specifically designed to utilize her four min arms. Flinn had been surprised to see a member of his race among the colonists, but not enough to mention it to the young female. Even so, Diyanna was growing frustrated at Flinn's insulting attitude.

"You appear wanting to make a statement," she finally snapped at him. "Please speak freely."

"This equipment; it is archaic. It is a wonder electricity still runs through it."

"And what would you know of our monitoring and processing equipment? Are you a miner yourself?"

"I come from a family of miners. That is what we are known for. Perhaps you have heard of us, the Lor'an of Inso."

"No, I have not heard of you. Should I have?"

Flinn blinked several times and stepped back. "But you are Vas'nolo. All on Inso know of my family."

"Not I," Diyanna shrugged. "My ancestors came to Sandicor almost three hundred years ago. I was born here; I have never been to Inso."

"It is your homeworld—"

"*Sandicor* is my homeworld."

"Not really."

"No, really!"

Flinn recoiled. "You are quite emotional. Are you suffering from a vitamin deficiency because of poor diet and lack of starlight on your skin?"

"My diet and skin are fine! Why are you even here? Do you not have better things to do?"

Flinn looked again at the equipment in the room. "I was curious. The Corve 418 Definer is much faster than what you have here and can detect more minute amounts of particulate. I am surprised you have not upgraded since … since never!"

"If you have not noticed, we are a poor community. This equipment has been here since the founding—"

"I can tell."

Diyanna glared at the young Vas'nolo male. "It still functions, and it is all we can afford. I suppose you are so rich that you never have to fix anything. All you do is buy a new unit and throw out the old."

"I am only trying to be constructive. If you upgraded, you could refine more particulate and even other varieties of materials other than just E-129. My family mines hundreds of elements and minerals that are used across the galaxy. We also have interests in the reactors that produce *artificial* E-129. There is much potential in your colony if you had the right equipment … and operators."

"What is wrong with the operators?"

"Nothing. You accommodate what you have available. I am sure it is the best you can do."

"That is correct! I would like to see you maintain and operate this equipment as I do. You would not know the first thing to do … except possibly to call an expert. And an expert you are not! And should I remind you, if it were not for Chanco and his thieves, Sandicor might be able to upgrade—as you call it. As it is, this is all we have. It is all we have ever had."

Nanni approached Flinn from behind and laid a spindly hand on his shoulder. The alien jerked when touched by the grey alien, having heard the stories of what Nanni could do with his internal electricity glands. He was in the room with Flinn, fascinated by the electronics within the colony. As Flinn had so indelicately pointed out, everything was a relic; however, it was used in such a way that the community functioned —and quite well, in Nanni's opinion.

He'd watched the interaction between the pair of Vas'nolo from across the room, studying the dynamic, amused by the young male's lack of awareness of his actions. For a being that utilized electricity in a variety of ways, Nanni could tell there was *electricity* between the two. However, his teammate was blind to the connection.

"My friend, Flinn, have you upset this young female of your species, and for what reason? Can you not see she is prideful of her skills and equipment, and now you have insulted her."

"All I did was tell her the truth. Why is that an insult?"

"Because it is!" Diyanna yelled.

"The truth is an insult? That appears to be more *your* fault, not mine."

Diyanna's skin was growing darker by the second, and her eyes were wide and intense. Eventually, she waved one of her six hands at Flinn and turned back to her duties.

"Leave now. Minos is in pre-eruption mode, and I have much work to do. I do not have time to play tour guide while suffering your insults and insinuations. Unless you want to serve at a station, go. Both of you."

Nanni pulled Flinn out of the room. In the hallway, he leaned over and said, "I am not a Vas'nolo, so I cannot be a judge ... but am I correct in assuming young Diyanna is a fair specimen of your race. A rare find in this part of the galaxy."

"By fair, you mean appealing ... in a sexual way?"

"That is exactly what I mean."

As they walked, Flinn looked back at the door to the control room. "I would imagine; I have not given it any thought. My mind is on the mission."

"That is good, but are you not also consumed by instinct? Members of my race can sense sexual energy at far distances. We mate rarely, but when we do, it is dynamic; it is magical."

Flinn grimaced. "Why are you telling me this? The mating habits of aliens are of no interest to me."

"I am not speaking of *my* mating habits. I speak of yours."

"Mine? I have no mating habits."

Nanni sadly shook his head, giving up. "That, my friend, is obvious."

16

Alarms were going off throughout the complex.

Adam and his mercenaries rushed from their rooms, not in panic but for excitement. The coronal eruption had just occurred on Minos, and the planet was within two minutes of being drenched in the first bath of deadly radiation and heat.

Tansin had invited the team to view the event in his private chamber adjoining the Grand Hall. Since the colony was expecting the CME to take place within a three-hour window, Adam was already anticipating the alarm. He was at the Grand Hall in twenty seconds and ready for the show.

Tansin's workroom was large—as were all the rooms in the colony, with polished stone walls of red, grey and black. The striations within the walls were beautiful and mesmerizing, but it was the huge monitor that drew Adam's eyes immediately. Various cameras operated on the surface, shielded against the intense heat and radiation, beaming live to hundreds of screens throughout the complex. When the first waves struck, it was like an Aura Borealis but made of yellow and white, dancing in the air and across the surface, taking on a life of its own. Adam didn't know how hot it got outside, but it was obvious it was in the thousands of degrees. The rocks trembled while some shattered. The air itself seemed to explode, with popping sparkles of intense light that temporarily whited out the screens. The scene was both hellish and heavenly at the same time.

The team stood silent, gawking at the twenty-foot-high screen, broadcast in such stark detail that it was like being on the surface. The harder Adam stared, the dizzier he got, having to look away to the sides of the monitor just to regain his bearings.

Fortunately, the initial shower only lasted about ten minutes before the sky calmed and the air stopped popping. Exhausted for some reason, Adam turned to Tansin. "What now?"

"Now we wait. The ejecta is traveling out from the star at many thousands of miles per hour. Even so, it will take approximately seventy hours to reach Sandicor. And be warned. The ejecta carries much more mass than the radiation. There will be violent tremors and disturbing sounds coming from the planet. You will think we are being torn apart. But be assured, Sandicor has felt millions of such bombardments, and still it exists. We will survive this next one."

Tansin was called to take a link. He listened for a moment before turning to his guests with a beaming countenance.

"We are indeed entering a very active period for Minos. Initial measurements have this current event even stronger than the last. Not only that, but the density of the ejecta is greater. It should be a bountiful harvest, and the tremors I spoke of, they should be even more pronounced. It shall be quite the experience for you."

"In seventy hours?" the huge monster Raccs asked.

"Yes. That is when it will begin. But the eruption itself lasted several minutes, which on a stellar scale means tens of thousands of miles. The rain should last for five to six hours. That is why the harvest will be so rich. There will be more time and material to catch."

"And Chanco will know," Vinset stated.

Tansin turned serious. "A stellar event like this is impossible to hide, especially when he will be looking for it. He will also know by the intensity that the harvest will be one of the best—if not the best—in the history of the colony. He will come for his share."

"But it is not *his* share," Flinn said firmly. Then he waved a hand at the rest of the team. "That is a lesson we are here to teach him."

Tansin shrugged. "If his kind is capable of learning."

After the coronal mass ejection—the CME—the colony returned to normal for the next three days. They weren't in the business of collecting radiation, so the initial blast was inconsequential to them. However, as the speeding cloud of stellar ejecta neared the planet, the miners began to put on their game face. Adam noticed the stark change in attitude. As amateur warriors, they seemed confused, uncoordinated and slow to learn. But in their element—as stellar miners—they moved with utmost confidence and skill.

Although the collectors were huge, they only covered an insignificant speck on the starside surface. This meant there were incredible amounts of E-129 that simply struck the planet and was absorbed into the soil. On other planets around similar stars, mining operations were designed to extract the E-129 from billions of tons of extruded surface material. These facilities were massive, usually contained within football-stadium-sized crawling machines that scraped the surface and then filtered the rock and debris through giant graters. As impressive as the operation on Sandicor was, surface mining was magnitudes bigger. And much more expensive.

The miners of Sandicor used a different approach, a more passive means of collecting E-129. The colony was started on a budget, and it never matured much beyond that. Over the years, the natives *did* upgrade their equipment, contradicting Flinn's critique. But they chose to spend the money on improved collection grids rather than computers and filtering machines. At the time, those upgrades were also planned, with funds being set aside for the improvements.

And then Chanco discovered the colony. And now, he'd been coming to Sandicor for four years, just when Minos was beginning its latest—and most productive—phase in its life for CMEs. Just when the colonists could have made real progress in securing their future, they were sent backward. Within two years, all the reserve credits were gone, and then each successive harvest put them farther behind. The existence of the colony—although seemingly content and comfortable on the outside—was reaching a fatal critical mass. The failure of the power module just before the first eruption of the season showed how vulnerable they were. If they'd lost a third of the harvest—and Chanco took most of what was left—there wouldn't have been enough credits for the colony to feed itself or import the other critical goods that living on Sandicor required. As little as two months ago, the colony on Sandicor could have died.

Instead, it got a reprieve. For how long, that remained to be seen.

Adam didn't wait for the alarms to sound this time. The arrival of the ejecta was a more precise calculation—it was the timing of the initial eruption that was an estimate. But the natives knew to the minute when the first traces of stardust would begin raining down on the surface of Sandicor.

Adam and Vinset had journeyed to the airlock at the top of the access tunnel stairs Suma had shown them thirteen days before. Here they could witness the arrival through eight inches of specially designed glass in the airlock hatch. Although the window was shielded from the full intensity of the event, the mercenaries were advised to take additional eye protection. This event could be one of the biggest to hit Sandicor in the life of the colony.

Adam had seen movies with amazing special effects portraying the Earth being struck by a coronal eruption. That or a gamma-ray burst. Both were equally devastating—planet killers. And now, to be separated from such a catastrophe by only metal and glass was thrilling—and a little foolish.

And then it began.

The initial burst was slightly anticlimactic, with only a thin cloud of charged particles and stellar dust raining down on the rocky surface like a strong downpour on Earth. And then it tapered off to nearly nothing, promoting Adam to look at Vinset and say, "Is that it?"

It wasn't.

Suddenly, both beings were jostled by a rolling earthquake, followed by a deluge of dark material shooting from the sky. Adam couldn't call the debris *falling* because it was hitting the surface much faster than the planet's gravity. This stuff was coming down in buckets and at easily three hundred miles per hour.

The rumbling continued, as did the bombastic roar from outside. It was a symphony of horror, reverberating through Adam to his very core. And Vinset had an even harder time coping with the deafening sound and flashing light coming through the window.

"I ... I must go. This is too intense."

And then he was gone, racing away from the airlock and down the stairs.

Adam wasn't afraid, not after the initial shock faded. Now he was mesmerized. Acts of nature had always fascinated him, even as a kid. He loved watching videos of volcanos and hurricanes, even earthquakes, which were prevalent where he grew up in Southern California. Of course, he never had to live through the major events he watched, not like the poor victims. And now, he was as close to being in the eye of a tornado as anyone could imagine. A tornado and a volcano all wrapped into one.

As he gained confidence in the barrier protecting him, Adam pressed his face as close to the window as he could, cocking his head to see as much of the hellish landscape outside as possible. He was amazed at the volume of material striking the planet until he realized this was just a shrug to a star, a tiny burp spewing out such a small amount of mass that it wouldn't be noticed. At least on the scale of a star. On a planetary scale, it was a different matter.

Adam remained in the airlock for the full forty minutes of the main display. The material would continue to rain down on Sandicor for several days to come, but this was the main show. Adam's heart pounded, and he felt as if the hair on his arms was standing on end. It probably was. A fair portion of the display was made up of static discharges caused by the charged particles interacting with the atmosphere. The whole of Sandicor was charged like a Van De Graaf generator and would remain that way for weeks, painting the sky over both hemispheres in a brilliant aura that would put Earth's to shame.

When the show was over, Adam reluctantly made

his way down the long stairway. Now that it was over, the next chapter in Adam's latest adventure was about to begin. Now, he had to wait for Chanco.

17

Three days later, Nanni noticed Flinn come from the collector control room, a place he was surprised to see him exit.

"I was not aware you were welcomed in there again," he said as he slipped up beside the young alien. Flinn picked up his pace, but Nanni stayed in stride.

"The refining process has begun. I was simply offering my assistance based on my years of experience."

"Is young Diyanna on duty?"

Flinn nodded.

"And she welcomed your … input?" Nanni had to suppress a laugh at his ribald reference.

"I know what you mean. Please do not make it more than it seems. It was innocent … and your fault."

Nanni recoiled with a smile. "Mine? How so?"

"It was you who drew my attention to Diyanna. As you remarked, it is rare to find members of your race this far from the homeworld. There are twenty-three Vas'nolo on the planet, derived from three bloodlines, and now all related in one aspect or the other."

"That could prove to be problematic under traditional mating practices."

"What is traditional?" Flinn asked defensively. "You are well-traveled. You know the variety nature has found."

"I have, and I do. So, I would imagine the introduction of a fresh bloodline would be welcomed."

Flinn stopped and turned to glare at the grey alien.

"You are assuming much. And besides, the situation is impossible. I am only a visitor here. Once our mission is done, I will be moving on to other challenges and other adventures. My destiny is among the stars, working alongside beings like you and the Human. The thought of spending my days—"

Flinn stopped speaking when the pair was joined by Adam, Jornay and Raccs.

"What are you talking about?" Adam asked, having noticed the intensity of Flinn's expression. But then, his expression was always intense.

"Nothing—" Flinn said quickly.

"Our friend has a potential mate," Nanni amended.

The three other mercenaries grinned at an embarrassed Flinn. "Is that so," Adam asked. "You don't waste time, do you?"

"It is not what you think. We are only friends."

"Friends with electricity," Nanni laughed.

"To you, *everyone* has electricity!" Flinn barked.

"It is a fundamental force in the universe. Accept it, my friend."

Adam patted Flinn's shoulder. "Don't mind him. We're all jealous of you. We're a diverse group. You have to find opportunities when—"

Adam was interrupted by a message coming through his ear mic. All the mercs were fitted with them as the time got closer for Chanco's arrival.

"Advance-Three has picked up two ships inbound on a trajectory common with Chanco." It was Vinset on the link, reporting from the central comm center. The mercs were taking turns monitoring the station. A day after the eruption shower, three small survey craft were launched and placed some distance from the planet as an early warning system. And now, contact had been made.

"Estimated time to Sandicor, four hours."

"It has only been three days," Jornay pointed out. "We were told he usually comes five to eight days after an arrival event."

"He must be anxious to get his hands on the harvest," Adam said. "He could see this was a big eruption. But don't worry; we're ready; in fact, I'm itching for some action."

The aliens looked at Adam quizzically, working through the literal translation. By now, most of them didn't question his strange speech patterns. Instead, they let the comments slide and used their own judgment as to what he meant to say.

"Okay, let's get the natives to their stations. We know what to do." He grinned and bounced an eyebrow. "It's game time!"

18

The planetary wind was still cutting sharply across the metal pads at about twenty-five percent higher than its normal speed when Chanco brought his two ships in for a landing. Sandicor was still cooling down from the latest drenching of star-hot plasma and would be for several days to come. But according to projections, it wouldn't cool much. Minos was gearing up for a series of massive ejections, a prospect that made Chanco grin with excitement. His other activities weren't bringing in the revenue they had in the past. It took a lot of credits to maintain his operation, with many mouths to feed. Only Sandicor was turning a decent profit.

As always, the raiders' ships weren't lowered into the receiving chamber below. This was by design. Chanco didn't want his vessels locked in an underground chamber, reliant on the natives to let him out. Not that he feared the miners; it was just habit by now.

To transit to the underground community, each ship had a snaking umbilical tunnel that would mate up with an access hatch located about forty feet away. Chanco used his own linking tubes, again not wanting to rely on local resources. He wanted to come and go as he pleased, here and elsewhere.

The tubes ran out and connected to the access ports before being pressurized. Then the airlocks were opened, and his troops began to move through. Chanco had forty-eight raiders with him for this trip, each wearing dual MKs and with about a third also having Xan-fi rifles slung over their backs. In the four years he'd been coming to the planet, his bandits had never had to use the weapons, and now they were here mainly for intimidation purposes. Only Chanco had taken the lives of the miners, and that was on his initial visits, to teach the colony who was in charge.

Once in the lower receiving cavern, the troops split up, with a third coming with Chanco to meet with Tansin while the others fanned out into the community looking for valuables to take. The finds were getting scarce, and in the overall scheme of things, their value wasn't much. But it helped appease the savage nature of his crew as they had their way with the natives, feeding off their fear and suppressed anger. It took a certain type of individual to be a raider. And Chanco's troops were the best at what they did.

As Chanco's entourage left the hangar, they encountered a work crew of miners chipping away at a huge pile of rock and debris that had fallen from the ceiling. The air was filled with a hazy greyness and smelled musty. Cave-ins, such as this one, were common in the colony, especially after such a powerful set of flares had hit the planet over the past few months. This path was blocked, but another was open. Without breaking stride, Chanco led his troops down the smaller tunnel to the right.

Only a hundred yards down this tunnel, they encountered another cave-in. The workers stopped what they were doing and gawked at the intruders, silent in their protests and concerns. Chanco kept an even countenance, not bothered by the looks. Like the rest of his raiders, Chanco fed off the anger and welcomed the fear. It was one of the reasons he chose this life path. It satiated a primal desire he had to dominate all that was around him, be it living or environmental. Some would call it a sickness; Chanco called it an advantage.

As always, the bandit leader's eyes were keen and darted from side to side and up and down. Like any wild animal, he shunned enclosed spaces. And now his routine was being disrupted. At a third change of direction, Chanco felt the tips of his stubby horns begin to heat up. He was getting angry, which only heightened his senses even more.

Eventually, Chanco came out at the main concourse again and near the Grand Hall. He relaxed, knowing where he was. Even here, the air was foul with dust. He had been coming here for four years, and this was the most damage he'd seen to the underground community. This also increased his caution. Could more tunnels collapse while he and his raiders are here? It was a very real possibility.

He turned to Laznor at his right.

"Contact the others, tell them to forgo the scavenging and return to the ships. I do not feel we are safe here. The tunnels appear unstable."

Laznor nodded and then began speaking into a hand communicator. Not all the bandits were linked for sound, but the lieutenants were.

Chanco pushed his way through the double doors leading to the Grand Hall. There were a few miners here who stopped to watch the raiders enter. Chanco motioned for three of his entourage to join him as he entered Tansin's office, including Laznor, who was just finishing up his calls, leaving the others in the auditorium.

Tansin was seated at his desk, flanked by the young miner he'd seen before. His name was Suma. But it was the being seated to Tansin's left that immediately drew his attention. It was a smallish creature with pink skin and short, yellow hair and blue eyes. Chanco was experienced enough to recognize the species. It was a Human.

Chanco motioned for the others to cover the door while he scanned the room with his eyes for others. And then he began to nod.

"I have suspected ever since the four bodies of my crew were discovered on Nefar. I had inquiries made, where I learned that you—Suma—and two others from Sandicor had met with an alien." He laughed. "I do not think it was you, Suma, who killed my people; they were too skilled, and you are too weak." Then he focused his dark eyes on the Human. "It had to be you. But how you accomplished the task by yourself is a mystery … and a warning. Vor was one of my toughest and most skilled fighters; however, his head had been nearly cut off."

Then Chanco turned to glare at Tansin.

"What have you done, my friend? Why have you introduced this variable into our very accommodating arrangement? It will only bring you grief and pain. Now, all I ask is that you give me what is owed to me, my share of the E-129. Judging by the strength of the flare, it was even larger than the last one. The harvest must have been rich, enough that you could afford to hire this Human."

"It was," Tansin spoke, almost shouting. "Over one hundred units. And no, I will not turn it over to you.

For far too long, you have ravaged our community, bringing hardship and despair to all who live here. That has come to an end. Your presence here is no longer tolerated."

Chanco grinned and cocked his head. "And how do you intend to stop me, Tansin? With one tiny alien? Yes, I have heard of Humans, but it would take a whole army of them to defeat my force, and I do not see an army in this room. I see only one creature. Are you, Human, going to stop me … all by yourself?"

A door on the other side of the room opened, and a non-descript grey creature with long arms stepped out. "He is not alone."

Another door slid open, and a third alien appeared, taller than the Human but also slender, with yellow hair and blue eyes.

"There is more here than you see," he said. "In truth, the Human has many friends and allies, more than you know."

Chanco frowned at this third alien. "Do I know you? You look familiar." Then he shrugged off the distraction. "You should know that not even three will deter me. Even if the miners gave up their entire harvest, they could not have hired enough of you to defeat my army. "

The Human slowly rose to his feet, a thin grin on his face and a sparkle in his eye. He displayed no fear, an emotion Chanco could instinctively sense in others;

in fact, the tiny creature seemed to be almost enjoying this moment. Three aliens against Chanco and his three lieutenants. The bandit did not consider the two natives in the equation.

Chanco glanced down to see the single MK strapped to the Human's leg, noticing that it had additional bulk and attachments he was not familiar with.

"So, is this it, Human?" he asked. "You intend to face me, possibly kill me? And what will you gain? You will surely die at the hands of my troops, after which they will tear this place apart, taking all the 129 and everything else." He turned to Tansin. "You may be right, my friend. This may be the last time I come to Sandicor. After today, there will be nothing left to return to."

"I don't think this is going to turn out the way you expect," the Human began, "Tansin brought me here to give you a message, a message you've already anticipated and rejected, from the look of things. But I'll still give you one chance—one chance only. Take your thieving gang of slimy degenerates and leave. Leave now, take nothing with you, and never return."

"And if I do not?"

Chanco gasped as the Human drew his weapon faster than any creature he'd ever seen and had it leveled at the raider's chest and only inches away. Bensin and the others had their weapons out as well, but long after the fact.

"Wait!" Chanco ordered.

He studied the weapon and the strange additions it carried. There was a lower section that was foreign, but the top part of the device was a standard '88. The alien's trigger finger was on this section, and the weapon was set at Level-2.

Chanco grinned. Then he glanced over at Laznor, who met his eye and then lifted the communicator so he could see it. Good, the link was still open to his lieutenants outside the office. They heard everything.

"If he wanted to kill me, he would have done it already," Chanco stated. "But he is concerned about the backlash."

The Human laughed. "That is where you're wrong, Chanco. I *do* intend to kill you; in fact, it will be the highlight of my day."

"Then why have you not?"

"Because I want to savor the moment. I get such satisfaction when I kill an alien asshole like you that I don't want to rush the experience."

"Then proceed!" Chanco growled. He stepped closer to the Human until the barrel of the weapon was against his chest. "Do it! I don't think you have the—"

The flash bolt lit up the room and splashed into Chanco's chest, sending him tumbling backward. But Adam didn't get a chance to savor the moment as he wished. Instead, the door to the office burst open, and a dozen raiders poured in, flash weapons blazing. Adam dove behind Tansin's desk while Vinset and Nanni ducked back into their respective side rooms, returning fire as they did. Tansin cowered in fear, while Suma had an MK-17 out and ready for action.

Adam lined up on one of the three bandits who entered the room with Chanco, laying him out with a shot center mass. And then Nanni was at the side doorway, firing. Adam had never seen him fire an MK before, and now he was stunned at what he saw.

The grey alien had an MK-17 in each hand and with a near-constant stream of bolts jumping from the barrel. First ten, then twenty bolts, filled the room, driving most of the raiders back out into the Grand Hall. And these bolts appeared to be Level-1s. The weapon was not rated for that, with a battery capacity of only five shots at L-1. But then Adam noticed the glow from Nanni's hands. They were literally electrified, feeding power into the weapons and recharging the batteries at the same time. In theory, Nanni's guns had unlimited ammunition as long as the alien himself remained charged.

And Vinset was also holding his own, firing a single weapon with deadly accuracy and speed, not relying on the targeting computer. In addition, if a raider came within range, Vinset would send out his whip-like twelve-foot tongue to slap at the enemy soldier, either distracting or blinding him, depending on where the tongue was aimed. Then Vinset would take him out with a blast to the chest or head.

The battle for Sandicor had begun. The word was out, with ambushes taking place throughout the colony and with his other three mercenaries coordinating the attacks.

So far so good.

But then it seemed as if there were even more raiders at the doorway and trying to force their way in. They were brazen, almost manic in their attack, not concerned for their own welfare. Something wasn't right.

And that's when Adam was struck with a Level-2 bolt in his side. He spun around, grimacing at the burning pain, ready to kill the bastard who just shot him. And then he froze.

It was Chanco.

The bandit leader was on his side, a light haze still in the air from when he'd fired his weapon at Adam. The alien's eyes were wide, and his mouth open. And he was alive.

But Adam shot him, point blank, in the chest. Was Chanco a creature also immune to lower bolt charges? And then Adam saw other bandits moving, lifting themselves off the floor to resume the battle. Besides the possibility of the dead miraculously coming back to life, there was only one other explanation.

"They're wearing diffusion vests!" both Adam and Chanco yelled out in unison.

But only one of them was right. Adam survived the deadly flash bolt because he was a Human. Chanco survived because he was wearing a *diffusion vest*.

There was a momentary lull in the battle as both alien and Human looked at each other. And then Chanco ran, crouched down and covered by a canopy of his soldiers, each laying down suppressing fire, keeping Adam and his mercenaries at bay.

The office cleared out as the bandits took their leader and ran. There were still dead raiders on the floor, having been struck in the head or limbs and succumbed to their injuries. But it was only a handful. Most of the enemy force was still intact.

Adam was on his throat comm.

"They have on diffusion vests," he repeated on the open channel. "Give me a status."

"Yes, we have noticed!" Raccs' booming voice cried out through his mic. He was stationed at one of the artificial cave-in locations leading to the hangar chamber. There were eight natives with him who had qualified with the MKs, along with a dozen who were there just to lay down suppressing fire.

"I have told the natives to aim for the head," Raccs continue to report. "They are doing their best, but the bandits know they are immune to most of the shots. They are regrouping for a counterattack, attempting to get to the hangar room."

"Fall back to tunnel eight if you must," Adam ordered. "We're moving out of the Grand Hall. Our bandits are moving to tunnel nineteen. We're going after them. And by the way, Chanco is still alive."

Raccs bit his bottom lip in frustration. The plan—as the Human had explained it after repeated translations—was to cut off the head of the viper and then leave the rest without guidance. It was a sound plan until Chanco failed to die. Now, the raiders had a purpose for remaining. They had to help their leader escape.

Raccs peered over the pile of red rock. There were five dead raiders on the floor, but the remaining cluster —about twelve of them—were in plain sight and seventy feet away. They knew the limited range of the MK-17 and what lousy shots the natives were. They also had confidence in their vests, and that was why, with a battle cry that made Raccs jealous, they began their charge.

Raccs had one of the rare Xan-fi rifles. He was a decent shot but by no means a master. He preferred his battle ax and fists to this modern mode of killing. Still, he was able to take out three more bandits with headshots before he began aiming for their legs. Once one went down, it was easier for the others to saturate his body with flash bolts, hoping one of them would hit a vulnerable area. Even so, Racc's position was about to be overrun.

"Fallback to tunnel eight," he commanded, barely getting the word *'fallback'* out of his mouth before the miners abandoned their posts and ran away. Only a few were headed for tunnel eight.

"This is Flinn in the merchant's section. We have killed nine bandits, but the others got past us, moving through the shops to open ground. We are in pursuit."

The merchant section was the commercial district of the colony, where private enterprises were run featuring specialty goods. The fake barriers had been set up at either end but not in the district itself. That would have been too disruptive. But now, the enemy had swarmed past the first barrier and entered the mall. Most of the shops were linked through back tunnels, and the raiders were using those to move through.

Flinn had all four of his K-90's charged, yet he only carried one in his hand. He hated to admit it, but the Human was right. In the heat of a battle with multiple targets, he could only concentrate on one at a time. He'd taken out three bandits that he knew of, but that was mainly due to the power and efficiency of the '90s targeting computer. Still, it was better than any of the natives had managed. Although they had the drop on the raiders initially, once it was discovered that most of their shots were ineffective due to the diffusion vests, it turned into a free-for-all with no plan to speak of. Flinn was with half a dozen natives, moving from store to store, looking for bandits. Or … were the bandits looking for *them*.

A blast struck the miner directly on Flinn's right. The Vas'nolo dove for the floor, and then using his six arms and two legs, he scampered away as fast as a normal being could run. At a point, he slid on his stomach on the polished floor, under a display case and came up, drawing one of his weapons as he did.

He was behind a pair of bandits crouched behind a display. They didn't know what hit them as Flinn placed accurate bolts into the backs of their heads in rapid succession, again utilizing the blindingly fast speed of the weapon's targeting computers.

That made five, just by himself. He wondered how the others were doing.

Jornay had lost his weapon a while back when the raiders charged and then took up a defensive position at the debris mound just abandoned by him and his natives. He'd scrambled back to get it but was driven back by a barrage of bolt fire. When he returned to cover, his troops were gone, nowhere to be seen.

This was in one of the tech sections of the colony, with a myriad of rooms and portals of astounding variety. This played into Jornay's strengths. He was able to jump to higher levels and then slink overhead, lining up on a target below.

Once a single raider—or even a pair—came within range, he would drop onto them and sink his two-inch-long claws into their exposed flesh while ripping with his needle-shape teeth. It was quick and bloody, and then he was up again and moving away.

He'd taken out five raiders so far, but now it was getting more difficult. He was soaked in alien blood and leaving trails everywhere he went, making it possible for the enemy to close in and coordinate their attack. With no other option, Jornay leaped to an appropriately named catwalk and sprinted away deeper into the complex while surrendering an escape route to the raiders.

Chanco had started with approximately sixteen soldiers in his party, and as far as Adam could tell, he was down to nine. The Human, Vinset, Nanni and Suma were in a mad dash after them—a mad dash for the aliens, a leisurely stroll for Adam. But he couldn't get too far ahead of his backup. He'd taken a flash bolt to the side, a hit that had set his shirt on fire and scorched his entire left side. The cloning had stepped in—as it always did in situations like this—and helped dull the pain. He would be completely healed in a couple of days.

But for now, he sprinted around debris piles and down tunnels, thinking what a clusterfuck this had turned into. The plan had worked perfectly, right up to the point where the bandits didn't die when shot, at least not all of them. Even so, Chanco was paying a high price for his visit to Sandicor. Perhaps it would be enough to teach him a lesson. Unfortunately, Adam was having trouble convincing himself of that.

From reports Adam was getting, the bulk of the raider force had made it back to the hangar cavern and was waiting for Chanco. That put Adam and his mercenaries in jeopardy, seeing that it was now only them—and Suma—against the bandit force. Even if Adam caught up with Chanco, they couldn't do much more damage than they already had. So, when they reached the hangar, Adam had his people take up defensive positions and not advance. Going into the chamber would have only gotten some of them killed.

Flinn, Raccs and Jornay soon joined the others, watching on monitors in the hangar bay control room as the bandits regrouped with Chanco in command. The mercenaries had tried to open the topside doors and evacuate the cavern of air, but the raiders had overridden the systems. They were in there for the duration or until they decided to leave.

Adam took a quick count of the surviving bandits, as best he could tell. There were twenty-seven of them, which was a sizeable force since they now knew what they were up against. There seemed to be a debate taking place on whether or not to mount a secondary strike, to reenter the colony and kill every last miner they saw. Tempers flew, as displayed in facial expressions and hand gestures. The outlaws waved their guns, working themselves up for another battle, a scorched earth campaign to the end.

To Adam's surprise, it was Chanco who was the calming factor and the voice of reason. Although he couldn't hear what was said, he watched as Chanco spoke, taking command of the horde. And then, after about ten minutes of further debate, Chanco pointed to the access hatch and sent his soldiers toward the exit. He was the last to enter the tunnel, and before he did, he looked back into the cavern and looked around until he found one of the surveillance cameras. He stared into it for a moment, knowing Adam was looking at him. And then he gave some strange salute, a sweep of his hand across the burnt fabric of his shirt and then a palm raised outward.

Adam didn't know what the gesture meant, but he imagined it was some kind of a tribute to a fellow warrior. Or it could have been the alien's way of flipping him off. Yeah, that was the more likely meaning.

19

It was a miracle that none of the mercenaries were hurt or killed, which made it even more embarrassing that Adam was the only one who got shot. Still, that was a minor consolation. Although they managed to kill twenty-one of the bandits, seventeen natives lost their lives in the battle.

The colony was in disarray, with the wailing of mourning families echoing off the stone walls. But that only lasted for a few hours. Soon, a new spirit circulated throughout the lava tubes and caverns.

They won! They'd driven Chanco away. And they'd also managed to keep all the refined E-129 from the last flare, a staggering one hundred six units, the most ever recovered. The credits they could get for that would help rebuild the damaged colony and do so much more. And with the prospect of keeping all future harvests, the mood of the natives changed dramatically.

Two days later, Adam and his mercs were called into the Grand Hall, which was filled with natives, as many as the auditorium could hold. Suma was on the stage with Tansin and a couple of other miners, and the colony leader was in the middle of praising the efforts of all the natives but calling special attention to the three with him. They were given medals of some kind—probably something made up on the spot—to commemorate their heroism.

When Adam and his people entered, the entire chamber stood, and an incredibly raucous and painful cacophony of alien cheers filled the Hall. Adam winced as the sound nearly pierced his eardrums while it insulted his taste in music. Damn aliens can't sing; not a single one of them. And that made their various forms of cheering sound like a gaggle of wailing cats.

But Adam didn't complain. Tansin soon quieted the throng and invited the six mercs onto the stage. *Is this where we get cheap medals, too?* he thought. That's fine. This ceremony is more for the natives than for the mercenaries. And besides, Adam knew a tragic truth, one he was reluctant to share with the natives. So, for now, he would smile and enjoy the festivities.

"My very good friends, please step forward," Tansin began, beaming with pride and energy. The old miner had to be feeling pretty good. He barely survived the shootout in his office two days before.

"On behalf of the colony, I want to thank you all for the magnificent job the six of you have done."

It wasn't the Magnificent Seven, but it was the Assorted Six, Adam corrected in his mind.

"We now realize the value of the services you offer your employers, services that often come down to life or death. Honestly, before now, we did not respect those who would have need of beings like you, believing each should fight their own battles and not pay to have others fight them instead. It seemed to be a cowardly means to an end. But now we understand. Sometimes, events dictate drastic measures. And my friends, you are the drastic measures Sandicor needed."

The damn crowd cheered again. Adam looked at the others and noticed that only Jornay seemed as bothered by the screeching decibel level in the room as he was. It had to be that their ears were more sensitive.

"But now, please, may I have quiet."

Answering Adam's prayers, the crowd fell into an anxious hush.

"But now, having time to evaluate your contributions to the colony, it has been decided that a portion of the harvest from the season's first flare—the amount that would have been spent on a spare power module—shall be instead offered to the six of you as bonus compensation for your selfless act."

Adam opened his mouth to speak, an instinctive reaction to being offered something he didn't think he deserved. But then he stopped when Vinset leaned over to him and whispered, in no uncertain terms, "You better not. We deserve fair pay."

Adam gave the alien a tiny smirk and nodded. He was right. They all needed the money, some more than others.

"And how much would that be?" Adam gasped as Flinn nonchalantly asked in front of the entire colony.

Tansin blinked several times. "The amount has been worked out, but I believe it is around two hundred eighty thousand energy credits in total to be split among you. Power modules are not inexpensive."

The math was a little harder for Adam to do in his head, but he figured it to be around forty-eight thousand each. Compared to the three million credit bounty Adam got for Warden Zankor, forty-eight kay was a drop in the bucket. But to the other mercs—all except Flinn—it was a fortune. Gratitude was on full display on the faces of Raccs, Vinset, Jornay and Nanni. Adam smiled, too, working to keep his teeth from showing too much. There was no telling who might take offense to his unintentional death challenge.

"And now, what are your plans, my friends?" Tansin asked.

Adam had discussed it with the team.

"First, we're going back to Nefar to pick up a few supplies. And then the team is breaking up. And now, because of your generous bonus, many of us will have new destinations and new adventures to look forward to. We thank you, thank you all."

Adam grimaced as he finished the little speech, knowing what response it would elicit in the chamber. Fortunately, they were led into Tansin's office while the cheering continued, with the door muffling the godawful noise. Suma came with them. Apparently, he had been elevated to a co-leadership position within the colony. Adam approved; he deserved it.

The credits were already counted out and placed in rectangular holders on Tansin's desk.

"Please, take your share," Tansin said. "I only wish it could be more."

The team thanked him.

Then Adam took Suma's hand, placing it in his, and then shook it. "Human's official gesture of thanks," he explained to the young miner. "I'm glad it all worked out. It was touch and go there for a while." Adam caught himself as he saw the frowns on the assorted alien faces. "It means that for a while, the outcome wasn't certain."

Suma nodded. "On that, we agree. But in the end, it did."

"So, what's next for you, Suma?" Adam asked, anxious to hear of his promotion.

The alien beamed.

"First of all, I am to lead a delegation to Nefar. There, we will sell the new harvest, and then—should I say—we will purchase a new power module with the profits. I pressed for paying you the bonus as a gesture of appreciation, knowing paying it would not hurt the colony's finances."

"It is still appreciated," Vinset said. "More than you will ever know."

Adam smiled. Forty-eight thousand credits wasn't nearly enough to buy a new spaceship, but it would help Vinset recover from his recent bout of bad luck. That's if he doesn't lose it all again in another card game on Nefar.

"Is there any other news?" Adam prompted, baiting the young miner.

"Indeed, there is. Upon my return, I will become the new leader of the colony as my good friend Tansin has decided to relinquish his post."

"Retiring?" Adam asked Tansin.

"I understand the translation, and in a way, I suppose. But no one in the colony truly retires. There is always a job we can do until our last breath. I will continue to serve."

"Good for you."

Adam then turned his attention back to Suma. "I discussed this with the team earlier, and we want you to know that we have voted you a member of the team, the seventh member of what I want to call *The Magnificent Seven*. You will round out the count. Congratulations."

Suma didn't react the way Adam expected. Instead, he looked at Adam's share of the energy credits still on the desktop. "Does this mean I share in the bonus?"

Adam hadn't thought of that, but a quick look at the faces of the original Assorted Six gave him the answer.

"I'm afraid not. Sorry. It's more of an honorary position. Besides, you have to be a member of the Mercenary's Union to get paid for services rendered."

"I have not heard of such an organization. Can I join?"

"Only if you make your living as a mercenary."

"In that case, I shall refrain. But yes, I am highly honored to be included in such esteemed company."

Adam was relieved. He didn't know how much longer he could keep lying.

The team then moved in and congratulated Suma, willing to do so now that they knew he wouldn't be taking any of their reward.

Since both the miners and the mercenaries were

going back to Nefar, it was decided they would have a going-away celebration at the bar on Nefar where Adam and Suma first met. It had only been thirty days since that time, and a lot had happened. But the end was near, and unlike his past few missions, Adam was coming out the winner. He had a bonus forty-eight kay in his pocket, plus his pay for bringing in Zankor waiting for him back home. He was feeling pretty good about things. His finances were recovering, and he wasn't being hounded by Tidus about returning the company's starship to the home base. The *Arieel* was now his. And he could take her anywhere he damn well pleased.

But for now, it was the short hop over to Nefar. He wouldn't be there for long before heading home to Tel'oran. Adam caught himself. Since when did he start considering Tel'oran his home? Just now? Had the miner's special connection with their planet and colony rubbed off on him? Was Adam Cain, *the alien with an attitude*, getting sentimental? Homesick?

Adam shrugged off the confusing emotions. This was just another mission on another speck somewhere in the vast Milky Way galaxy. Even so, as he lifted the *Arieel* from the surface of Sandicor, he amended his last thought. Adam Cain was a man *without* a home. But he did have a starship.

And that was just cool as shit.

20

It had only been a few hours since Flinn, and the others had left Sandicor, and already Diyanna was missing him. Since losing Juhana, she had been lost, confused. Life on Sandicor was hard enough, but to add *lonely* to the mix was almost too much to bear.

Perhaps, having now experienced a little of what the rest of the galaxy had to offer, she might venture out, possibly go to Nefar or one of the other major hub planets. There was much more to life than the colony—

Her voice inhaled at the thought. What was she thinking? The colony was her home; more than that, it was her family. It wasn't only the other Vas'nolo; it was everyone. And now her good friend Suma would be leading the colony. And without the threat of Chanco continually hanging over their heads, perhaps the galaxy could come to Sandicor. With the promise of rich harvests in the future, Sandicor could prosper, adding new facilities, new resources, possibly even bringing a music venue to the planet. Diyanna enjoyed music, but there was so little good music on Sandicor. With their newfound wealth, she might advocate for such an improvement. Others would welcome it as much as she.

Diyanna was in Palace Three, looking out through the crystal walls at the varied sky. To her left was the yellow light of Minos, low in the sky and casting long shadows from the Salonin Mountains and cutting the glare from the Lifegiver. To her right, she could see the cold blackness of space with its sea of stars twinkling through the thin atmosphere. The Rasnin River flowed from the cold side to the temperate zone, spending its entire life within a three-hundred-mile zone where liquid water could exist. Some of the river's flow was channeled into the Peace Palaces, creating miniature rivers inside the domes and feeding the grasses, trees and bushes that grew within.

The trickling of the nearby waters brought a soothing calmness to Diyanna's soul, which was the purpose of the Peace Palaces. No matter how claustrophobic or depressed a colonist became, they could always find solace within the Palaces.

And yet ... she still missed Flinn.

"Attention on Sandicor!"

Diyanna was at first startled and then confused by the voice that boomed from the speakers within the Palace. The other colonists in the dome at the time felt the same way. The sound was being channeled from the colony's communications center, but it was not the voice of a colonist. They all knew the voice; it had haunted their dreams for years.

It was the voice of Chanco Kantos.

"I am very disappointed in your recent actions, so much so that I could not dismiss my anger without taking action. It is obvious that you do not understand the significance of my involvement with your colony—with our colony. I have heard the protests when I include myself as a colonist. But it is true. I am of the colony. But more than that, *I am the colony*.

"And now you have betrayed me and killed my soldiers. You have insulted me and brought pain and anguish to the families of those you had slaughtered by your hired killers. But I do not fault the mercenaries for what they did; that is what mercenaries do. They kill. It is you who I hold responsible. And now I will prove to you how vulnerable you are ... to me! I will prove to you that I *own* this colony, that I am your *leader*, I am your *god*. You will serve me, or you will die.

"In ten standard minutes, I will destroy the three

Peace Palaces. I will give those of you within the structures time to leave, not because I am soft, but because I need your labor to harvest my E-129. Once the Palaces are destroyed, I will go, returning at the next harvest. But the destruction of the domes will be but a precursor to what I can and will do if you ever betray me again. For next, it will be your precious collectors that I will destroy. And without them, there is no colony.

"Keep that in mind the next time you complain about how little of the E-129 I leave for you. I leave enough to keep the colony functioning; that is enough. It is time you realize that I am your master, that you work for *me!* Do as you are told, and the colony will survive. I may even give you a little extra E-129 from time to time to help improve your living conditions. However, if you ever question my authority again, I will destroy the collectors. I will take away your reason for being on Sandicor. I will let you die.

"Now, you have ten minutes to vacate the Palaces, starting now."

Diyanna ran off for the nearest exit along with the thirty-five other colonists who were in Number Three at the time. *This is horrible,* she thought as she ran. They had fought Chanco in order to free themselves of his yoke. Instead, they only made it worse. There was no pretending any longer. If Chanco wanted to destroy the Palaces and the collectors, he could do it from space, and there was nothing the colonists could do to stop him. It was hopeless. There would be no new prosperity for Sandicor, no fresh music wafting down the corridors or through the speakers. A dark cloud had suddenly descended over Sandicor. There would be no happiness here for a long time to come ... if ever.

Diyanna would leave. Yes, she would leave Sandicor and make a better life for herself elsewhere.

But what of her family? What of her fellow colonists? Could she leave them, only adding to their burden during the harvest and for maintaining the colony? Then a thought struck her, tying her stomach into knots. *Will Chanco even allow me to leave?* If too many colonists left, there wouldn't be enough of them to process the harvests. The E-129 yields would drop ... and Chanco would not be happy.

No, she could not leave, even if she wanted to. She was imprisoned on the planet, just like everyone else. Chanco would see to that.

21

The *Arieel* was still eight hours out from Nefar when Adam received a panicked link from Suma's ship.

"A horrible thing has happened on Sandicor!" the young miner exclaimed. His face was flush, and his eyes flowed with tears as Adam watched the scene on the comm screen. Vinset and Flinn were on the bridge with Adam, with Flinn's tiny speeder in the cargo hold.

"Is it Diyanna?" Flinn jumped in to ask. "Was she hurt?"

Suma shook his head. "She is well. It was she who linked. But it is the worst news possible. Chanco has returned."

Adam grimaced. This was the unspoken worry he had from the beginning but wasn't willing to vocalize. Even if the mercenaries were able to drive Chanco away, he could always come back. And the sad truth was that most of the time, the bad guys came back ... unless they couldn't.

"Go on, Suma," Adam said. "Tell us what you know."

"Chanco returned ... and then he destroyed all three of the Peace Palaces. He blasted them from space; there is nothing left."

"Casualties?"

"None. He gave time for the domes to be evacuated. But that is not even the worst of it. He has threatened to destroy the collectors if we do not submit to his absolute rule and dictates. He spared those in the Palaces so there would be more slaves to harvest his E-129. He is taking command of the colony and all the E-129. He will only allow us enough to live on. And if we protest again, he will destroy the collectors and let the colony die. This is ... this is ..." Suma broke down crying.

"We must go back! We must help!" Flinn yelled out. "This cannot be tolerated!"

All eyes were on Adam, who sat strangely quiet in the pilot's seat. After a moment, Vinset spoke, reading Adam's reaction.

"It is over. We did our job. It is time to move on. We are not responsible for the consequences of our actions. We were paid to fight, and fight we did."

Although his words were true, there was a lack of sincerity within them.

"We cannot do nothing!' Flinn cried out, confused by the stoic reactions of the Human and the noncommittal words of Vinset. Even Nanni was silent. The mercenaries—the true mercenaries—knew the truth.

Flinn glared at his teammates before steadying his eyes upon Adam.

"This fits within your philosophical profile of pragmatic mercenaries. You said it before; this is not our fight. We have no *'skin in the game.'* And if we went about caring for our clients, we would lose eventually. This is one of those moments. Is that why you sit there silent? This is what you believed all along would happen. We would drive Chanco away once, but then he would return."

"It's what bad guys do," Adam confirmed. "That's why they're the *bad* guys."

"And I thought we are to be the good guys, to use your Human slang."

"We are the guys who were hired to do a job." Vinset inserted. "Nothing more. It is not our fault that you found a more personal tie to the colony. That was all your doing."

The anger flared in Flinn, even more than he was already experiencing. He was still wearing his M-90s, and his four main arms went for them.

It was so fast that Adam couldn't see it, but in a

split second, Vinset's tongue lashed out and removed the weapons from Flinn's trembling hands, tossing them to the deck. And then it wrapped itself around the young Vas'nolo's neck and began to squeeze. Not a lot, just enough to get his attention.

"Everyone calm down," Adam ordered.

The tongue receded, and Flinn began rubbing his neck, staring at Vinset, his eyes on fire. Then he bent down to get his guns, and Vinset shook his head. "Leave them there, for now. Let us see how this game plays out."

Adam nodded, knowing that Vinset sensed something in Adam's quiet demeanor. In fact, his mind had been racing, working through scenarios and having an internal debate as to the right course of action. In the end, Adam Cain did what Adam Cain always does: He picked the worst possible course.

"Where is Chanco now?" Adam asked Suma. The link was still open, and the miner had watched the conflict between Flinn and Vinset, aghast that there might be shooting taking place on the bridge of the *Arieel*.

"Diyanna said he left for Nefar as soon as he destroyed the Palaces. He is returning to his base."

"Okay," Adam began with a sigh. "I only see two options. One, Chanco takes over the colony and holds the threat of destroying the collectors over your heads for decades to come. Or, two—" He paused. "Or two, we attack Chanco on Nefar … and we kill them. We kill them all." Adam turned to his mercenaries and shrugged. "I'm going with option two. Who's with me?"

"Promise me they'll be no conciliatory speeches or offers of surrender," Vinset said. "If we see a bandit, we kill a bandit; if we see Chanco, we kill Chanco."

"That's the plan. And another thing, they'll be no reason for the raiders to be wearing diffusion vests at their base. They should go down a lot easier than they did on Sandicor."

Adam's and Suma's ships had linked up, and planning began for the raid on the raiders. Suma had a total of six colonists aboard, and each of them had proven themselves in battle, being some of the most worthy warriors Sandicor had to offer. That was good. In addition, all of the mercenaries agreed to join the fight, especially Flinn, whom Adam turned to at an all-hands planning meeting.

"We may need some extra weaponry, something a little more powerful than MKs and Xan-fis. Some portable flash cannon would come in handy."

"There will be no problem. I will get those for you, along with diffusion vests for all of us. Give me a list, and I will get it for you."

Adam nodded. It was good to be insanely rich, obviously.

"Vinset, you're the only one of us who has been to Chanco's town. What can you tell us about it?

"It's called Grendin. It is not very big. The Sixty-One ribbon runs by it, but a smaller road connects with it from the ribbon. There is not much there. I believe the village once produced sulfur powder and a small food crop for the paste masters. It was subdued the only time I was there with very few people on the streets."

"And the inhabitants? Are they friend or foe?"

"I was not there long enough to make a determination. I would assume they live in fear, as does anyone who comes in contact with Chanco and his raiders."

"And where is his headquarters?"

"Grendin lies at the end of a small mountain range, and Chanco has appropriated four grand manors on the hillside overlooking the settlement. He occupies the structure on the largest expanse of flat land on the hillside. Some of his troops are housed in the two adjoining homes."

"And the fourth?" Nanni asked.

Vinset laughed. "That manor lies higher on the hill but has a smaller footprint on the hill. Being not as grand as the central home, Chanco has left that one vacant so no one can command a residence higher on the hill than he."

Adam pursed his lips and nodded. "A vacant home on the high ground; it has potential. We're going to need detailed maps of the area along with aerial photos. Also, an accurate head count of the raiders. When we go in, it will be a blitzkrieg operation." Adam was ready with an explanation of blitzkrieg. "A lightning strike, fast, clean ... and merciless. As Vinset has requested, we go in to kill and don't stop until there is no one left to kill."

"That could be a problem," Vinset said. "There is a landing field on the opposite of the village from the hillside where Chanco keeps his spacecraft. There will be raiders there as well as the manors."

Adam thought for a moment. "You're right; that could be a problem with his troops split. But I think the main concern about the airfield is keeping his ships from taking off and providing air cover. We'll have to take out the ships while they're on the ground while at the same time attacking the homes. I guess we all know that the *kill them all* statement was a generality. We're really after Chanco."

"Along with as many of his raiders as we can dispatch," Nanni added.

"Of course."

Adam noticed a small string of saliva drain from Jornay's mouth. The cat being was stimulated by the prospect of unrestricted violence and the free flow of blood. Then he noticed Raccs mirrored the emotion on his massive square-jawed face. Secretly, all the mercenaries—including Suma and his miners—were feeling the same unbridled passion for death, so long as the death was confined to Chanco and his soldiers.

Good, Adam thought. *Keep them fired up. They'll need that energy to carry them through the hell they're about to experience.* Adam had been through far too many similar actions in the past that he felt he had more insight than the others. It was going to be bloody ... and costly, with most of them not returning from the mission.

Adam knew it was a stupid, impulsive decision to attack Chanco's base with only a handful of fighters. It was also diametrically opposed to his credo as a mercenary ... *to always come home.* And to never make a mission personal. But then he recoiled, trying to think of a mission where he *hadn't* taken it personally. Scouring his memory, he realized it was his pride or concern for others that got him into the most trouble. And that went back as far as he could remember. In the final analysis, Adam Cain was nothing but a bleeding-heart softy who let emotion govern his actions, everything he'd warned Flinn not to do.

How do you spell hypocrite? Adam thought. And then: *Seriously, how do you spell it? Does it have an 'i' or a 'y', two 'p's or one?* He wasn't sure. Spelling wasn't one of his strong suits.

But killing bad guys was.

22

It paid to have a wealthy young hothead on the team. Flinn attacked his assignment with a single-minded fury, sparing no expense. He seemed to have a bottomless bank account and could call on favors—even on Nefar—based on his family name.

The first thing he did was rent a warehouse in the town of Tanic, about twenty-five miles from Grendin. It would serve as the staging area for the operation. Then he brought in two large trucks for hauling equipment to and fro. He had a list, including four shoulder-mounted flash cannon, top-of-the-line three-barrel Xan-fi rifles with extended range, along with K-90s for everyone. If they were going up against a vastly superior force, then they needed to have the best equipment. And Flinn was willing to get them the best money could buy.

Intelligence was gathered from various sources, but mainly from the ubiquitous Library. It could access the local databases of thousands of worlds, drawing information from files when needed. Being a modern world, Nefar had a myriad of satellites surveying the planet around the clock, with most of this surveillance available to the general public. But even as the photos and videos came in, Adam was still in need of hard intel acquired by boots on the ground. He needed to know the true count and location of the raiders, both at the spaceport and on the hillside. He also needed to know the demeanor of the Grendin natives. Data records put the population at one thousand nine hundred forty. Not a lot unless they were all in for Chanco. That was something Adam needed to know before he launched a full-scale assault on the bandit. Would the citizens of Grendin rally to help Chanco … or Adam?

At the drop of a hat, there was a rented transport at Adam's disposal for the trip into Grendin, courtesy of Flinn's bank account. He took Vinset with him, along with a survey telescope that could see much farther than binoculars. He needed to survey the spaceport and the hillside from the same location. The last thing he needed was to be spotted watching the village. Chanco was already suspicious enough, and the only way the operation would succeed was if Adam and his mercs struck first, struck hard and with overwhelming force. He couldn't afford another diffusion vest fiasco like on Sandicor.

Grendin was in a small depression at the base of a forty-mile-long mountain range. The hill on which the raiders resided was called Radnok Mount, and across the town, another small hill arose before tapering off into flatlands that extended all the way to Anacin. The spaceport was at the base of this hill, being nothing more than a large flat area where spacecraft could land.

Adam and Vinset drove the transport to the Anacin side of the smaller hill and parked it under the canopy of a grove of native trees. They climbed the short distance to another patch of trees before stopping to set up the telescope. It was computer operated and linked to datapads, both on-site and in the warehouse in Tanic. The scope was hidden in the shadows, allowing Adam and Vinset to remain behind the crest of the hill and out of sight from either the town or Chano's manor.

Adam worked the controls, first aiming the telescope at the spaceport located only three miles away. As the lens focused, Adam and Vinset shared a look.

"There are four ships," Vinset verbalized.

"Commercial vessels, along with Chanco's?" Adam theorized.

The scope zoomed in, able to distinguish individual rivets on the dirty hulls. Using the controls, Adam scanned the vessels.

"No commercial markings, no company names," Vinset pointed out. "And they are each of different makes, the customary sign of pirate and raider vessels. They take what they can get."

Adam had already reached that conclusion.

"He came to Sandicor in two of the ships," Adam said. "Does that mean he has a second crew, maybe troops he leaves behind? Until this last trip, going to Sandicor was a cocktail cruise. There was no need to take his whole force."

"If you mean it was easy, then I concur. We killed nineteen of his Sandicor contingent, believing he only had twenty-seven fighters left. We may have miscalculated."

The team at the warehouse was wired into Adam and Vinset's conversation.

"This matters not!" Flinn barked. "We must carry through with our plans. Chanco must die."

Adam looked at Vinset and smirked. They all knew Flinn's obsession with taking out Chanco and protecting Sandicor. But he was right. This didn't change the overall objective, just the details.

Adam continued sweeping the landing field, pulling

back on the field of view from the telescope to get a better overall view of the port. There was one large hangar and two smaller outbuildings, all of which had seen better days. Metal sides were rusted, and a few windows were broken. He began a count of the people he saw on the ground, of which there were quite a few. In addition, none of those he saw were Nefareans. Adam hadn't seen any of the bull-like natives among Chanco's crew, so he had to assume everyone at the spaceport was a raider. He counted sixteen, working on the spaceships, loading or unloading cargo or just milling around. If all Chanco had were twenty-seven bandits, then that would leave only eleven on the hillside. Adam guided the telescope toward the manors to check it out.

The powerful scope was able to get a decent view of the distant buildings, zooming in to pick out individual beings, both outside and through windows. Already he could tell his count was off. Just a quick scan of Chano's manor and the two homes to either side showed twenty-five others, not counting those he couldn't see inside the homes. Even though the count was now over forty, Adam had to double that to be safe. If two of his vessels could carry approximately fifty troops, then he should have around one hundred bandits, minus the nineteen left in bodybags on Sandicor.

And then a thought occurred to him. Vinset came

to Grendin to interview for a job with Chanco. With the loss of life on Sandicor, there was a good chance the raider was already rebuilding his force. He had been back on Nefar for four days, which was long enough to get the word out. And not all interviewees would have the same sense of morality as Vinset. They would jump at the chance to join the gang.

So, at least a hundred fighters, not counting any support they may get from the town. Adam rolled over in the grass and stared into the sky, something that caught Vinset off guard.

"What are you doing?"

"I'm thinking; give me a minute."

Flinn was right, Adam thought. The main objective is to kill Chanco—something Adam thought he'd done on Sandicor. But this time, he had to make sure it stuck. The idea was to hit hard and take out the leader in the first wave. In the meantime, Adam's twelve-being force could do a lot of damage with flash cannon and the element of surprise against the troop buildings. Then he thought of the spaceport. The *Arieel* could take out the four ships as long as they remained on the ground, and he could strafe them from a low approach before they knew what hit them. And then, with command of the air, the *Arieel* could have a significant impact on the ground battle.

But they would have to be sure they take out Chanco. Undoubtedly, his estate was equipped with panic rooms and possibly even escape tunnels, and at the first sign of trouble, he'd make for them. Adam was hoping for a blitzkrieg attack, and if he had to dig around through rubble to find Chanco's body—living or dead--that would give the raiders time to recover and for the townsfolk to join in if they were going to.

That canceled out the use of the *Arieel* on the main home. He could level the side buildings, leaving his people to concentrate on the main estate. And in the overall scheme of things, the population of Grendin didn't count. His troops wouldn't be on the ground long enough for them to mount a counterattack, not if killing Chanco was the objective.

Adam decided on a two-prong attack. One: Take out the spaceport with the *Arieel*. Even if some of the bandits survive, it will take them time to reach the hillside. And Two: Simultaneously, the other eleven members of his team would move down from the vacant home at the top of the hill and assault the main structure. They could also keep the soldiers at bay in the side homes long enough for Adam to hit them from the air. But then he'd have to land to join in the fight. And join he must. He was *The Human*. He couldn't let a good battle go to waste.

Adam surveyed the pile of armament and equipment at the center of the warehouse. Flinn had outdone himself. He seemed to have doubled up on everything, which made Adam start thinking about stashing some extra K-90s in the *Arieel*. They could come in handy on future missions.

And there were diffusion vests specially designed for the various species. Diffusion vests are essentially coils of wire that channel the energy from a flash bolt and spread it out, allowing the force and heat to dissipate rather than penetrate the body. They were effective—for one bolt. After that, they were useless. Unless you have backups, and Flinn had provided plenty. The problem was how to carry extras and then have the time to put on a new vest in the heat of battle. It was a possibility, and Flinn's intentions were good, if not that practical.

Raccs barked when he found the set of vests designed for him. He'd never worn one before, mainly because they didn't come in his size. But somehow, Flinn had found some that fit the monster. He literally giggled as he tried one on and then slapped Flinn on the back, nearly toppling him over.

"I thank you, my friend. May I keep this after the action?"

"It is yours; there are no refunds for a vest that size."

The rest of the team was sorting through the pile, claiming gear and weapons for their own.

"You have done well, Flinn," Adam said to the young Vos'nolo. Then on a more serious note: "Are you ready for this? You know this is going to get bloody."

Flinn always wore an intense look on his face. It was more intense than ever.

"I am. I know that we do this strictly out of vengeance, that all of us could have simply moved on. But I think you are wrong."

Adam frowned. "Wrong, about what?"

"About the heartless nature of mercenaries. Yes, many may fight simply for the credits. But I think others—like you and me—do the job out of a sense of morality, knowing what is right and what is wrong."

Adam nodded. "I think you're right. I've had to amend my thinking recently. Unfortunately, people like you and me don't last as long in this profession as do the heartless bastards who do it just for the credits."

Now Flinn laughed. "And you speak from years of experience. I understand from the others that you are older than you look, so for that, I will give you the benefit. And if that is true, then you contradict yourself. You are like me, and yet you have survived."

Adam winced. "You can't really say that, not if you knew the full story. But I have to admit, I'm really lucky, unbelievably so at times. In fact, I'm probably the luckiest asshole in the galaxy."

"Again, with the Human-speak. But as you said once, the longer I spend with you, the better I understand."

Flinn looked around at the rest of the team, spread throughout the warehouse, in good spirits with their shiny new toys.

"Then, shall we fight? Shall we seek immortality in our deeds? Shall we become ... superheroes like *The Human* for hire?"

"That's asking a lot, Flinn," Adam said with a chuckle. "I've been a superhero for a long time. It will take a while to catch up to *me*."

23

The battle would commence at first light, giving the team time to reach the hilltop estate under cover of darkness and then slip into position with the flash cannon to strike at the troop buildings.

The Human already had the *Arieel* in space and was biding his time until the rest of the team got into position. Vinset and the others took most of the night to reach the hilltop manor, using the numerous roads up Radnok Mount. At one time, four wealthy Nefarean families built and lived in the estates until two moved away, and the other two were made offers they couldn't refuse from the bandit leader. Now, the hillside was dominated by Chanco and his raiders.

The manor was dark and foreboding as Vinset moved his people closer, sweeping through open gates to enter the building. An electronic lock secured the front door, but Nanni made short work of it with his electric hands. He checked for alarms and found none.

From inside, they could see the other three homes down the hill. It was in the early moments of dawn, and the abodes were mostly dark, with only a few lights illuminating select windows. Even so, night vision goggles could make out a few sentries patrolling the grounds, finishing up a boring night shift, an activity that wasn't detailed in the Raider Recruitment Brochure. Vinset reasoned these had to be the lowest-ranking and the least-skilled soldiers of the group.

The eleven mercenaries were cloaked in non-reflective black and with cloth caps over their varied heads. Each was wired for sound, with throat mics and open channels.

Nefar had a pair of moons, but they were more like captured asteroids than legitimate companions. They didn't provide much light at night, surrendering that task to the whisps of star clusters that filled the sky the closer one got to the galactic center.

"Jornay, Nanni and Raccs, you are cleared to proceed," Vinset stated. With Adam in space, he was the unofficial ground commander. Adam would join them later if necessary. Hopefully, the team could make quick work of Chanco, utilizing the *Arieel* for evacuation purposes only.

The six natives from Sandicor were split between

Vinset and Flinn to help with loading the flash cannon cartridges. The cannon were shoulder-mounted and delivered a significantly more powerful plasma bolt on target, but they had to be reloaded after each shot. That's where the miners came in.

Vinset watched as Jornay, Raccs and Nanni moved out the back of the estate and down the hill, using natural rock outcroppings for cover in the lessening shadows of night. The Nefarean star was still thirty minutes from rising, but the sky was turning a pale shade of blue. The star would rise over the Mount at the mercenary's back while creating a blinding glare directly into the eyes of the enemy if they looked in that direction, as they would when the firing started.

Once the first three were off, Vinset took Suma and two of the other miners and moved to the left while Flinn and his team went right. They would place themselves in firing positions between the troop houses and the main structure, able to cover both targets.

Jornay reached the back property line to Chanco's home first, using his fluid, cat-like movements to his advantage. There was a security fence made of wire surrounding the estate, something that wasn't on the other homes. It was designed to keep the leader safe.

Jornay had already scoped out the back of the home with his night vision by the time Raccs and Nanni reached the fence.

"There is no one to the rear. Nanni, do you sense any ground or movement sensors beyond the fence."

Nanni shook his gray head. "I do not; it should be safe. Although the fence is active."

"Will that be a problem?"

Nanni grinned. "No. No problem; in fact, it will be stimulating."

"Very good," Jornay said. "Here I go."

Jornay then slipped off his shoes, revealing his long feet and retractable claws. They were as sharp as his front claws and, up close, were as deadly as any of the team's flash weapons. Then the cat creature settled back on his haunches and jumped, easily clearing the ten-foot-high fence and landing silently on the ground on the other side. He then sprinted to the back wall of the estate, moving to the closest window and looking in. He then turned and motioned to the others.

Nanni now reached out with his hands and grasped the electric wire. There was a light crackling and a smell of ozone, but nothing more.

"Go, Raccs," he said. "I can hold. But when I release the wires, an alarm will surely sound. But I will wait until I hear the signal."

Raccs already had his battle-ax in his gigantic hand, and he swiped down with it, easily slicing through eight feet of fence. He pressed his massive body through the opening and ran to join Jornay.

Jornay now had out a Tri-fi, a three-barrel version

of the classic flash rifle made by Xan-fi. As the name implied, it fired three bolts at a time along separate barrels. This negated the need for more powerful bolts since the plasma merged as it exited the barrels, forming a more destructive bolt with twice the range. Jornay had six extra battery packs strapped around his narrow waist.

Raccs also had a Tri-fi and eight battery packs. He also had his battle-ax and a diffusion vest. The giant felt even more invincible than usual.

With a nod, Jornay moved off to his left while Raccs went right. They were to assault the residence the moment the signal was given. And that moment was almost there.

After receiving word from Vinset, Adam dove the *Arieel* into the atmosphere. With the proliferation of starships throughout the galaxy, most planetary governments didn't regulate entries and liftoffs unless they were around populated areas or in designated traffic patterns for major starports. Adam was coming in hot but miles away from any city. He came from the north, a hundred miles from Grendin, before skimming the surface at barely a hundred feet elevation. He'd dropped into darkness only moments before he leveled out, but the plot was programmed into the nav computer, and Adam felt confident that he wouldn't encounter any unexpected obstacles. Even so, it was a wild ride, watching the ground rush by at just under the speed of sound. He didn't want to go supersonic and broadcast his approach with a thundering sonic boom.

The target was highlighted on the tac screen. He was only a couple of minutes out, with the flash cannon charged and his trigger finger loose. It would be like shooting fish in a barrel.

And there it was, the tiny spaceport. From orbit, he'd already verified that the four raider ships were still there and that none had lifted off during the night. Now he brought the vessels into a line on his targeting computer. He could have used the AI, but he always got a thrill out of firing the powerful weapons. It was more like being in a life-size video game.

And then Adam Cain unleashed hell on the ships below, spitting out eight bolts that streaked along the target line. Holes opened up in the hulls while plasma blasted the dirt field, flaring up to light up the early morning scene.

He was over the port in a second before banking to the right and whipping around the smaller hill to the west, the one where he first observed the spaceport.

Then he was on track again, firing at the ships in case any weren't damaged enough that they could still engage their defensive shields. But no screens were up, and Adam slowed some, taking more deliberate aim this time. The four spacecraft were blazing piles of twisted metal after his first two runs.

Then Adam circled around again, this time to target the buildings and foot soldiers. People were running, with a few on fire, as the hangar and outbuildings exploded. They weren't as sturdily built as the starships, so the cannon blasts literally vaporized the structures and anyone in them.

As Adam pulled the *Arieel* up to a higher altitude, he checked the aft camera. Daybreak had come early on this part of Nefar, manifested in the burning spaceport. And this was only the beginning of a very bad day for the residents of Grendin.

24

Nanni heard the explosions sounding from across the shallow valley. He released the fence wires, and as expected, alarms began to wail. The klaxons were unnecessary since the thundering blasts of cannon fire could be heard for ten miles in every direction. The inhabitants of the hillside neighborhood were already jolted awake before the alarms sounded, prompting the grey creature to grin. *Let the killing begin.*

Vinset had his flash cannon lined up on the northern flank of the troop building, waiting for the maximum number of raiders to show themselves. He knew Flinn was doing the same at the other house. It was a good bet that most of the raiders were in these two homes and not in the main estate. Chanco wouldn't want his home cluttered with smelly, obnoxious ground troops. That's why he gave them the adjoining buildings. Hopefully, that meant Nanni and the others wouldn't find much resistance.

On cue, panicked raiders began to pour from the buildings, propping up pants and awkwardly buttoning up shirts. Some even had diffusion vests fastened over their regular clothes instead of under them. They paused for a moment, gazing across the valley at the fiery scene at the spaceport, which gave Vinset and Flinn time to focus on the largest concentrations. And then they fired.

Bodies were blown apart, whether or not they wore diffusion vests. Weapons were spun around and pointed up the hill, but the mercenaries beat them to the punch with another pair of cannon bolts. More bandits died. Vinset snickered. *This is fun!*

Jornay slipped in through the unlocked front door to the estate, not surprised to find it unsecured; why lock it when there were soldiers coming and going at all hours? He immediately came upon a bandit who didn't notice him at first, assuming the cat-like creature was another raider; there were so many and of such a variety of species that it was hard to keep track. But then he paused, thought for a moment and then turned around. There was something odd about the way the alien looked at him...

That was as far as he got. Jornay jumped, coming down on the creature with both his hands and his feet, claws fully extended. The cuts went through cloth and flesh, some two inches in depth before Jornay locked his long muzzle on the soldier's exposed neck. The enemy soldier went down without a sound.

But then the foyer was flooded with another five bandits, all arriving from a stairway from below. They were armed and ready to fire, reacting to the wailing siren and the sound of explosions echoing across the valley. Jornay dug his claws into the now-dead soldier and held the body between him and the others as a series of flash bolts splashed into the still-warm and bleeding corpse. The force of the bolts threw Jornay back, where he landed hard on the tile floor at the base of a curving stairway going up. He cowered under the body, waiting for more bolts to come in. But none did.

He ventured a peek around the body, breathing a sigh of relief when he saw the hulking figure of Raccs grinning, holding his curved battle ax and towering over ten segmented body parts, two for each of the bandits from downstairs. Raccs had expertly sliced them in two with one swipe of his blade, eliciting an almost sexual glaze in the big alien's eyes.

"I thank you, my friend," Jornay said as he slipped from under the body. "But there will be more."

"I hope so."

And more there were.

A flash bolt streaked down from upstairs, barely missing Jornay. He spun around, leveling his K-90 at the attacker. He didn't wait to fire, not even with the superior targeting computer of the top-grade weapon. The powerful bolt—a Level-1—struck a four-legged creature in the lower abdomen, very close to his groin —if he had one—frying the skin and burning a hole through the soft-tissue being. The body tumbled down the stairs toward the pair of mercenaries.

"Stop playing around and find Chanco," a voice called out from behind Jornay and Raccs. It was Nanni, having entered the house from the back. "Go; I will secure the main floor," he said, indicating for Jornay and Raccs to clear the upstairs. It was where the bedrooms would be, along with the best views of the valley below. Earlier, the trio had celebrated their good luck of being chosen to lead the assault on the main house with the possibility of being the ones who killed Chanco. It was generous of *The Human* and Vinset—even Suma, who had more of a grudge against the raider. Now Jornay and Raccs bounded up the stairs, anxious to get the deed done. They could hear the flash cannon going off at the other two structures, and they had no idea how long they had before the area would be swarming with even more bandits than they could handle. Kill Chanco ... and then go home.

Nanni was momentarily distracted watching his teammates ascend the stairs, and he didn't notice the pair of raiders coming up from behind. A flash bolt went off, hitting the gray creature in the back—and on his diffusion vest. The force pressed him forward, but he didn't lose his footing. Instead, he whipped around and reached out with his exceptionally long arms, grasping both of the soldiers by their shoulders. Instantly, a powerful electric charge surged through his hands and into the bodies of the raiders. Nanni wasn't holding anything back. The shock was meant to kill. And kill it did. He let the raiders settle to the floor, smoke rising from their charred bodies, the scent reminding Nanni of a tasty meal and leaving his stomach growling. Nothing like charred flesh over an open flame to quinch a hunger.

But now Nanni whipped the Tri-fi from around his back, aiming the three-barrel rifle at another group of soldiers appearing from the stairway below. Nearly all the guards were coming from the lower reaches of the home, which made Nanni suspect that was where they might find Chanco. But before venturing down, he would wait for Jornay and Raccs to clear the upper floor. He might not have to run the gauntlet if they appeared with Chanco's head on a platter.

Adam had the *Arieel* streaking over the valley and gaining altitude to reach the crest of the hill above the top-most home on Radnok Mount. He had only been over the spaceport for a minute and a half, but it was long enough to destroy Chanco's raider fleet and kill a dozen or so of his soldiers. It was a good start.

From his ear comm, he knew the rest of the battle was proceeding according to plan. The two troop houses were on fire, with dozens of bandits lying dead or wounded on the ground outside or being toasted inside the building. For good measure, Adam lined up and placed two well-aimed flash cannon bolts into the house Vinset was firing upon. The structure literally exploded outward, showering the surrounding area with fiery debris.

"Ho! Why not some warning!" Vinset cried out in Adam's ear. "We are within the debris field."

"Sorry about that," Adam said. Yeah, two may have been one too many.

On Flinn's house, he only used one bolt, but it was enough to blow the top off the building and shatter every window. From his vantage point, Adam could still see around fifty raiders that survived, now ensconced in hiding places and returning fire on his mercenaries.

The enemy was too scattered and entrenched for his flash cannon to be effective without potentially harming his own troops. So, Adam spun the *Arieel* around and landed her at a pre-determined spot at the top of the hill.

With a K-90 and Tri-fi, Adam sprinted out the open airlock door and down the hill. As he approached, he noticed several vehicles were on the winding road leading up the side of the hill from the south. Others were filling the streets of the city. These were either natives joining or leaving the fight; he wasn't sure which. But from the look of things, the mercs wouldn't be on the ground much longer. He had three people inside the house and closing in on Chanco. This could be over in a few more minutes.

Adam ran along the side of the hilltop home before jumping a low brick wall at the end of the rounded backyard. He landed on the more radically sloped hill and stumbled, rolling a couple of times before he came back up on his feet and regained his balance. It was easier in the low gravity of Nefar, but still, he hoped no one noticed his falling. He was *The Human,* and *The Human* didn't fall.

He focused in on Vinset and his three miners as they huddled behind a rock, occasionally popping up to fire another cannon bolt at the raiders. With the houses gone, the remaining enemy troops had taken up defensive positions and were firing at both Vinset and Flinn. From Adam's vantage point, he could see a fair number of the raiders, and he opened up on them with the Tri-fi.

Whoa! He loved this weapon. It was a marked improvement on the old Xan-fis, which he'd been firing for nearly forty years. More power, better accuracy and longer range; everything a growing mercenary would want. Bodies flew, and the firefight began to settle down.

Adam settled in next to Vinset, discovering that one of the miners with him had been killed. That was expected. Even still, the pair of surviving miners in this group—including Suma—were having a hard time dealing with it. Although death was common on Sandicor, it normally did not come like this, through the use of flesh-burning plasma bolts, not until Adam and his people showed up at their doorstep. *Hey*, Adam thought. *No one said freedom was free. There's a price to be paid.*

"How are you guys doing in the house?" Adam asked over his comm. Things were pretty much wrapped up outside. All they had to do was find Chanco.

Jornay and Raccs were in the hallway traversing the upper floor. There were five doors leading off the corridor, two on each side and one at the end. Jornay was amazed at the internal size of the home, with twelve-foot-high ceilings common and doorways spanning five to six feet wide and ten high. Then he remembered that the homes were built for nine-foot-tall Nefareans with their four-foot span of deadly horns. The home had to be big and the portals to scale. This fit nicely with Raccs' massive size, although it made the much smaller and slinkier Jornay nervous.

They'd already checked the first two rooms, finding only one alien inside who unceremoniously met Raccs battle-ax. Jornay scolded him, telling the giant to use his flash weapons, warning that the enemy wouldn't always be within arm's length. The monster just snorted at him.

"We are moving among the sleeping quarters," Jornay reported to Adam. "Nothing so far."

They each took a door farther down the corridor, opening them simultaneously, ready for action. Again, nothing.

Jornay felt the hairs going up on his back. They'd only found one raider, and none of the rooms appeared to be used. Out of the four, only one had a bed, and it had no bedding.

As the pair met up again in the hallway, they looked to the last door, the one at the end that beckoned them forward. This was the room that would face out to the valley, the one with an expansive balcony, the one reserved for the Leader. If they were to meet resistance, it would be here.

And that's when Raccs hauled off and threw his battle ax at the door.

As expected, it shattered into a thousand pieces, releasing from the hinges in two spots. Raccs had his Tri-fi leveled, and now he charged, crashing through the few remaining fragments of the door and entering the room with a savage battle cry. Jornay was close on his six.

And then, just like the others, it was empty.

"There is a problem, Adam," Jornay reported. "We have cleared the upper floor, and Chanco is not here."

"Dammit," Adam said. "He must be in a bunker below."

"That is a given, but what is even more strange—none of the sleeping rooms have been used. Chanco never stayed upstairs."

Now Adam chuckled. "He's so paranoid that he always stays downstairs. It figures."

"We shall meet up with Nanni and begin the probe downstairs."

"We'll be in to assist in a moment. Just mopping up

the last of the resistance out here. But be warned; there are vehicles moving up the hill from the south. They should be at the hilltop in about fifteen minutes. We have to be out by then."

"What of Chanco?" Suma asked. "He must be found."

"I agree," Adam said. "But we talked about this. He probably has bunkers and escape tunnels below the house. He may already be gone. But we've destroyed his fleet and killed most of his troops. He's going to have a hard time regrouping enough to attack Sandicor again."

"But he will. He will make it his mission."

"Then you'll have to set up some defenses of your own. It can be done with shielding. And with the colony keeping all the E-129, you should be able to afford it." Then Adam smiled. "I would imagine the new leader of the colony might make that a priority once he takes office. And besides, we aren't through here yet. We may still find him cowering in a hole somewhere. I've seen it happen before."

Suma nodded. He wasn't happy with the answer, but it was better than nothing.

"Adam!" Jornay's voice was strained. "I am on the balcony; there is movement down the hill."

"What kind of movement?" He'd already noticed the increase in city traffic. Was this something different?

"The bad kind of movement. I see several of the raiders leading Nefareans up the road. They are coming in vehicles and on foot, at least a hundred of the natives and ten or more raiders."

Adam told the others to stay put, and then he ran off to the front of the building to look for himself. Sure enough, there was a whole caravan of vehicles moving up the switchback road, and they were about ten minutes out.

Well, that answers the question about whose side the city is on, he thought. And with more vehicles coming up the hilltop road, it was about to get very crowded around here.

"Okay, guys, I think it's about time to call it. There's a force of locals coming from below, and soon one from above. We don't want to get trapped—"

Adam found himself flying through the air, landing hard on the pavered yard to the south of the main home. His ears rang, and his vision was foggy. Stabbing pain covered his body, and he could tell part of his clothing was on fire.

He rolled, doing his best to snuff out the flames. Fortunately, he was wearing a diffusion vest that protected his flesh from the fire. He ended up on his side, looking back at Chanco's home, groggy and dizzy. Then he gasped at the horrific scene he saw. The home was gone, literally blown to kindling by an enormous explosion. Debris rained down on him, with torrents of black smoke twisting like a tornado into the early morning air.

"Jornay! Raccs! Nanni!" Adam repeated the call several times, each with no answer. The home was gone, and so were his teammates.

Then Adam called out to the others who had been clustered near the rear of the building. No answer, not until a weakened voice came through, barely recognizable as Flinn, fighting through agonizing pain.

"What happened?" the Vas'nolo asked.

"Chanco's house blew up. How are the others?"

"Let me ... let me check."

Adam was already climbing to his feet and staggering toward the back of the ... property. He couldn't say the back of the home because the home was no longer there.

"Suma, I believe he is still alive but badly injured," Flinn said in Adam's ear. "Vinset, I am not sure. His head is bloody. No one else is moving except me. I have suffered a broken arm. I have never broken anything before; this is excruciating pain, unbearable!"

"Yes, it is. Hang in there; I'm on my way."

"I will sit or lay, but I cannot hang. I told you I have a broken arm."

Adam knew the alien wasn't being funny, just literal.

It only took a few seconds for Adam to find the shattered remains of his mercenary force. They were located near the back of the property line, at a terrace wall about fifteen feet high that marked the end of the leveled section. A quick survey told Adam that four of the six miners were dead, with Suma suffering from extensive burns to his left side, and another miner—Anno—was moaning, his eyes closed, injuries indeterminant.

Vinset lay on his back with Flinn holding a piece of torn clothing to his head, trying to stem the bleeding.

"Is he alive?" Adam asked.

"Unknown, but the blood is still flowing."

Adam knelt, placing his head on the left side of Vinset's chest. Nothing ... no heartbeat! And then Adam remembered: *Vinset is an alien.* He moved his head to the other side of the chest. There it was ... a strong heartbeat, or what Adam thought was a strong heartbeat for the alien.

He was alive but unconscious and probably in shock. And the head wound meant a possible concussion.

"Are you injured?" Flinn asked.

"I'm fine. The vest protected me against the burns."

"Then you *are* a lucky asshole, as you have said."

"Do you remember everything I say?"

Flinn frowned even more than he was already frowning. "Do you not? The Vos'nolo have excellent memories. Now I ask, what of the others? They are gone, am I right?"

"Yeah, and we'll be the same if we don't get out of here."

Adam stepped back so he could see up the hill, fighting the glare of the morning sun. It was steep, at least until they got to the hilltop home, and with three unconscious survivors, it would be impossible to get them up there in one trip.

"Can you carry Vinset?" he asked of Flinn.

The alien grimaced. "Even without a broken arm, I doubt if I could."

Adam would have to do it himself, carrying one at a time.

"Help me lift Vinset. I'll take him up the hill to the *Arieel*—"

Adam fell back against the rock terrace as a barrage of flash bolts struck nearby. He and Flinn hunkered against the wall, protected by the slope from the shots coming from up the hill. The Nefareans had reached the hilltop home and were lying down suppressing fire as others of their kind made their way down the hill toward Adam and Flinn.

Adam pushed Vinset against the rock for more cover and then risked his life to pull Suma and Anno to cover, as well. Then he chanced a look over the wall. His eyes were once again assaulted by the rising star that was just now breaking over the ridgetop. For those down the hill, it was a major handicap—just as Adam and his crew hoped it would be, but for the raiders, not them.

Still, Adam lifted the barrel of the Tri-fi over the top and began lighting off bolts. The Nefareans were using standard Xan-fis; even so, they had a lot of them.

Then a shadow came over the mercenaries as the morning starlight hit a part of the hilltop home. Adam poked his head up and scanned the hill. There were about twenty to thirty bulls, with most at the edge of the higher property, shooting from behind the low brick wall. Five or six of them were coming down the hill to flank Adam's position, and except for a few lucky shots, there was nothing Adam could do to stop them.

Just then, another cascade of white-hot plasma rained down on them. Adam and the others only had about six feet of cover, so he and Flinn huddled close to the wall, cringing every time another round of bolts splashed nearby.

"Save yourself, Adam," Flinn called out over the muffled sound of the flash bolts going off. "You are a Human; you can escape to the side with your superior speed. It is time for you to *cut bait*, as you said. Time for you to come home alive."

Adam was thinking the same thing. If he stayed much longer, he'd be surrounded, and honestly, there wasn't much he could do to save Flinn and the others.

"I will cover your exit," the Vos'nolo volunteered.

"Damn, Flinn, you are hellbent on becoming a hero, super or not. Stop being so magnanimous. I'll probably leave, but I don't want to feel guilty about it."

"You mean after I am dead? The others will not see you leave them. It is acceptable. Go. We did what we could."

Adam looked to either side, gauging the distance before the property ended, and he could find cover within the natural terrain. There were rocks and gullies, along with a few trees. It would be tight, but it was better than staying here.

Adam took a couple of deep breaths, readying himself. And then he looked at Flinn. "I'm sorry, buddy. I wish there was more…."

Then Adam stopped speaking. There was something odd about the muffled puffs of the flash weapons going off. Although the sound and frequency of the puffs had increased, the splashing of the bolts at their feet was no more. If the Nefareans weren't firing at them, who were they firing at?

Adam stood up and climbed the wall again, chancing a look into the glaring sun. Indeed, the Nefareans were still firing while at the same time taking incoming bolts from off to the right. That's when Adam made out another group of Nefareans dressed in blue uniforms. Adam didn't know who they were; as far as he knew, the Nefarean army wore grey uniforms.

Either way, both sets of bulls were blasting at each other, but the civilians were far outmatched and outnumbered. There was a whole army of bulls on the hillside.

Then Adam picked up the stereoscopic sound of a battle raging all around, not only up the hill but down it. The cavalry had arrived, but instead of riding in on horses, the *bulls* were here to save the day … and Adam's Human hide.

25

Adam and Flinn stayed where they were, not wanting to become casualties of friendly fire, waiting for someone of authority to find them. It wasn't much of a stretch then when Warden Zankor strode around the burning husk of Chanco's home, a look of concern on his grey bull face.

He walked up to where Adam and Flinn sat, huddled near the recumbent bodies of Vinset, Suma and Anno. His face was serious, his black orbs burning into the Human.

"You are aware that it is against the law to stage an unauthorized military operation on Nefar?" he asked Adam seriously.

"I wasn't aware," Adam answered weakly. "I suppose now you're going to arrest me."

"I should, but I will wait for the results of the formal inquiry."

And then Zankor grinned. He looked around at the three burning houses and the clutter of bodies littering the hillside.

"You have made quite a mess, not only of the landscape but of yourself and your people."

"Can you help them?"

"Medical personnel are on the way as we speak. They will be taken to Anacin for the best medical care."

Adam now shook his head. "What the hell are you doing here?"

"It is a long but interesting story, one I must tell you someday."

"How about the *Cliff Notes*—a short version—right now."

More bulls were swarming around them, some with guns, others with medical cases. They moved in and began caring for Adam's injured. Carriers were brought in, and soon it was only Adam and Zankor left at the terrace wall.

"We have been watching Chanco's organization for many years," the Warden began. "However, he had always been under the protection of the former leader, Dalin. He would use Chanco and his pirates for various non-official operations of questionable legality.

With Dalin gone, I was planning a move against him, as well as Grendin. The settlement is one of the providences still loyal to Dalin and a hotbed of rebel activity. Laws and regulations against such activities are still being formulated by the new government. But when reports came in of a battle taking place in Grendin, I mobilized the quick strike force and flew here, intending to correct some past injustices on my own."

"Your form of *frontier justice*?"

"I know not what that means, but continuing, I spotted your ship from the air, realizing then that *The Human* was involved." He looked around at the damaged landscape. "I should have guessed beforehand.; your reputation for excessiveness is well known."

Adam ran a hand over the blue uniform of the bull.

"Do you like it?" Zankor asked. "We needed a new identity after Dalin. It was decided that blue was a good color for change."

"It works for me."

"Are you injured? Do you also need medical assistance?"

Adam shook his head. "Nah, I'm fine. I just want to get back to my ship. I'll fly it over to the spaceport at Anacin and then check on my people." Adam reached out and did the backhanded slap that was a Nefarean handshake, something he'd learned from Zankor. And then he began climbing the terrace wall.

"May I ask you a question before you go, now that I have saved your life?"

Adam stopped and returned to the ground.

He shrugged. "How can I refuse?"

"What is your name? The mystery has perplexed me since the first day we met."

"Why does it matter?"

"Indulge me."

"Okay; it's Adam Cain."

Zankor gasped.

"What's wrong?" Adam asked.

"You say, *Adam Cain*?"

"Yeah, what's the big deal?"

"Since our last meeting, I have been researching your Human race, as well as seeking more details on the Juirean/Human war. As you know, I am a student of galactic military history, and you stimulated my curiosity with mention of the war and the Dysion Void, among other things.

"It has been fascinating, my research, although what I now find more curious is that throughout the entire history, one name often reads prominently: Adam Cain. Surely, it must be a coincidence, a popular name among Humans."

Oh well, Adam thought. *Who cares if Zankor knows who I am? It's not like it's a state secret or anything.*

"Yeah, that's me. Adam Cain in the flesh."

"Surely, you jest. These references go back almost forty years and continue until only a few years ago. And even with your admitted trait of longevity, the fact that you are *young* does not support the contention that you are as old as you profess. You could not grow *younger* over time. However, I have seen videos and pictures; and you do have an uncanny similarity to this person Adam Cain. You can admit to me: He is your birth father."

Adam was getting ready for another lame excuse when Zankor made his proclamation. "Yeah, that works," he said enthusiastically. "Dear old dad, Adam Cain, Senior."

Zankor frowned, not understanding the reference.

Adam turned to climb the terrace. But at the top, he stopped and looked down at the towering bull.

"What the hell," he began. "Let me do you a favor, Zankor, for saving my life. I'm going to tell you the truth, the whole truth and nothing but the truth. But not here. When I get back to Anacin, let's have a meal together, where I'll tell you a fantastic story that you will not believe, but that every word will be true. As a student of history, it will fill in a lot of blanks for you, not only about the past forty years but going back three billion years. It's about how life in the galaxy came to be and how everything is intertwined. And again, every word will be true. How would you like that?"

"I would like that very much."

"You say that now, but after I'm done, you may think differently. It will blow your mind."

"I wish not for my mind to be blown. But if it satisfies my curiosity, then it will be welcome."

26

Adam worked his way up the hill, which was still filled with blue-uniformed bulls herding civilian Nefareans to waiting trucks. It looked as if the whole town of Grendin was being arrested.

He stopped in the backyard of the hilltop home and looked back at his handiwork. Four towering plumes of black smoke climbed into the morning sky, creating an ugly scene of death and destruction. And of loss. Nanni, Jornay and Raccs were gone, with Vinset's status unknown and Adam's adopted alien son, Flinn, nursing a broken arm. Adam really liked this team, probably more than most he'd worked with throughout the decades. He'll miss them.

And as usual, Adam was walking away with nary a

scratch. It didn't seem fair, but who was he to question the fates?

He entered the open airlock door to the *Arieel*, wanting nothing more than to take a long, hot shower before hopping over to Anacin. Yes, that would feel great—

Adam didn't see what hit him, but it felt like a heavy metal rod. It struck him mid-face, across the eyes. Blood gushed from cut skin, cascading into his eyes and blinding him. And then another hit, this one to his stomach, buckled him over. The final blow was to the back of his head, which had him tasting deck before he blacked out.

Adam came to quicker than someone with similar injuries, but it didn't matter. He was already in binds—one of his belts securing his wrists—and the seething figure of Chanco Kantos aiming an MK-88 at Adam's bloody and swollen head. His shirt had been ripped open.

"I knew it," Chanco stated, waving the gun now at Adam's chest. "That is why you did not die on Sandicor. If only you had, then we would not have all this, this waste!"

Adam could feel the steady drone of the *Arieel's* lifting jets, but the ship wasn't moving.

"Chanco?" Adam asked, feigning blindness.

"That is correct. And now, I am confused. You attacked my compound and destroyed my ships without provocation ... and without pay. Why? You are a mercenary; all you worship is credits. You do not fight for *causes*. In that way, we are the same. Except I also seek power. And now, you have made a terrible mess of my operation. It will take me years to rebuild. But when I do—and I can assure you I will—I was slaughter every last colonist on Sandicor. They started this; you knew nothing of me beforehand. All this death and destruction is on their ledger."

"Good," Adam said. "So, you'll let me go?"

Chanco laughed. "How can you retain humor at a time like this? No, I will not set you free. I will make the colonists pay, and you will go to the ground knowing I will."

Adam was getting better by the second, his cloning in supercharge mode. But he still wobbled slightly on the couch and squinted, making his injuries out to be more serious.

"What now, dickhead?"

Chanco frowned, confused, but he understood enough of the question to answer Adam.

"I have your ship—soon to be *my* ship—hovering at fifteen thousand feet. I intend to find out of Humans can fly. But more than that, I want you to feel terror before you die, not something as simple and quick as a flash bolt to the head. You will fall for several minutes, knowing you are to die and powerless to stop it. By the time you meet the ground, you will have gone insane."

"A minute," Adam said.

Chanco frowned. "A minute? What do you mean."

"I mean, I'll only fall for a minute before hitting the ground, not several minutes."

"How do you know that?"

"I was a SEAL; it was part of my training."

Adam watched as Chanco checked the translation of SEAL through the Library. A whispered code word was all it took to ask for definitions of words.

"Why would an aquatic mammal on your planet know of fall times from spacecraft?"

"We're a strange species."

Chanco got to his feet, waving the gun at Adam. "Stand up!"

Adam's wrists were bound in front of him, which was good; they could be used as a club. But Chanco stayed out of range, moving in behind the Human. The red-skinned alien pressed with the MK, directing Adam to make the short walk to the airlock. The inner door was already open, and he was shoved inside. Chanco followed, activating the outer hatch from a control panel on the wall.

The hatch cycled open, letting in the roar of the lifting jets as they burned, keeping the *Arieel* level and locked at fifteen thousand feet. The air was thin at this altitude, but they were still able to breathe. Adam could see past the city of Anacin and to the distant ocean. It was a pretty sight.

"Move," Chanco coaxed.

"Wait!" Adam said. He spun around to face the alien. "Don't you want to see the terror in my eyes as I fall?"

"Yes, I do. Thank you for the idea. Now, step backward."

Adam shook his head. "I don't think so. I'm not going to voluntarily walk out the door. I'm not crazy."

"Then I will force you—"

Chanco stepped forward, now within range of Adam's bound hands. The Human flicked his balled fists upward, striking the MK with such blinding speed and force that the weapon flew from Chanco's hand, bounced twice and then fell through the open airlock hatch.

Chanco was fast—for an alien. He now swung at Adam with a right cross, hitting Adam solidly in the jaw. It hurt, but not much, especially with Adam's body in cloning mode. Surprised, Chanco stepped back. He'd expected his hit to be a knockout blow. Instead, it made Adam smile.

"Welcome to reality, asshole."

And then Adam lashed out with his right leg. Chanco lifted his own leg to counter the kick, and that's when he learned the difference between bone from a light gravity world compared to that from a heavy gravity world—like Earth. Chanco's leg snapped, sending out an audible crack followed by a painful wail from the bandit leader.

He collapsed to the airlock deck, writhing in agony.

Adam stepped back and then used his teeth to unthread the belt, freeing his arms. He smiled down at Chanco, savoring the moment.

"What now?" Chanco groaned, echoing Adam's question from only a couple of minutes before. But he didn't punctuate his question with the word *asshole*.

"You know what," Adam began. "I kinda like the whole terror-for-minutes scenario you painted a few minutes ago, although it won't be nearly long enough for my tastes. But it is what it is."

"Wait!" Chanco screamed in panic. "You are a mercenary. You do things for credits. I have warrants from seven worlds. You return me, and you could earn millions. So you see, I am worth a lot to you alive."

Adam looked at the bandit and then at the open hatch. "Millions, you say? Just for turning you in? Wow, that sounds great."

Adam reached down and took Chanco's arm, pulling him up onto his one good leg.

"Can you stand?"

"Somewhat. But if you have a pain reliever aboard, I could use it."

"Sure, let me see what I've got."

Adam went to turn away but changed his mind.

"You know what, Chanco?"

The raider cocked his head quizzically.

"What?"

"Fuck the credits. I'd rather see you fly."

And then Adam kicked the alien in the stomach sending him flying through the hatch and into open air. Adam moved up to the doorway, gripping a safety handle as he looked down. Chanco's screams were lost within the roar of the lifting jets, but Adam could still see the flailing arms and legs, at least until the black dot that was the bandit leader was lost in the ground clutter.

"Watch out for the sudden stop, asshole!" Adam yelled after Chanco. "It's a killer."

EPILOGUE

Fourteen days later, Adam was maneuvering the *Arieel* to a landing on the metal pad above the Sandicor colony. He had a full complement of passengers, including a bandaged-up Flinn and Vinset. Suma was in the stateroom with bandages of his own covering a fair portion of his severely burned body. Modern alien medical technology had done wonders, and he was expected to recover completely. Anno, the same. Adam was scheduled to stay on Sandicor for a few days before heading for Tel'oran.

Vinset's injuries were worse than they looked, and he was out of the hospital in only five days. Still, he had a bandage as his head wound healed. It was the same with Flinn's broken arm. The young alien-of-wealth wore his injury like a badge of honor, basically scowling at anyone who saw him as if to say, "You should see the other guy!" Flinn was badass, so beware.

There were four body bags in the cargo hold containing the fallen colonists. The bodies of Raccs, Jornay and Nanni were never found.

The *Arieel* cycled to the hangar cavern below, where a congregation of colonists awaited. Adam opened the cargo bay door, and then the three surviving mercenaries went aft to receive their accolades. Not surprisingly, the mood was tempered by the removal of the body bags. Then before Suma could be wheeled away, Adam went up to the young alien.

"The colony will flourish under your leadership."

"Do you believe so? I am not so sure. Look what I started and all the death it has caused."

"You had to do it for a better future. Not everyone would have the courage to do what needs to be done. But you did. As we say on my planet, *'You da man!'*"

"I am?"

"Well, sort of. *'You da alien-man.'*"

"I still only understand half of what you say, but what I do understand I will forever treasure. If you ever come this way again, please stop and stay a while. You will be welcome."

And then Suma was wheeled away.

"He was a good soldier," Vinset said. "He will make a good leader." He was leaning against Flinn's tiny speeder, unconsciously rubbing the smooth hull with a hand.

"She's a beauty, isn't she," Adam said of the starship. It was small—it had to be to fit in the cargo hold. But it was fast and comfortable for one person … if the trips weren't longer than a week or two.

"This is just like the one I had, only newer," Vinset said. He looked at the rich alien kid and smirked, envious of Flinn's wealth.

Adam could read the sadness in Vinset's demeanor.

"I told you I'll see if I can get you on with Starfire, but no promises. Tidus really wants you to have your own starship."

"I appreciate that Adam, but the ride to Tel'oran will be sufficient. There I can find other work, maybe something where I don't need my tongue or my weapon."

"That's possible. It's a bustling planet."

Then Diyanna appeared on the loading ramp. She looked in and saw Flinn, with one of his many arms in a cast and taped to his body. She rushed up to him.

"Does it hurt?"

"Not much. I have had worse injuries."

"I grieve for you."

And then the pair of aliens did something with their lower hands, the ones that fed their stomachs. Adam took that as a Vos'nolo kiss.

Flinn looked over at Adam and Vinset before

letting Diyanna lead him off the ship. He stopped at the bottom of the landing, turned and tossed something at Vinset. The alien instinctively whipped out his tongue and caught it.

"What is it?" Adam asked as Vinset studied the object, his mouth agape.

"They are the controls to the speeder."

Adam and Vinset looked at Flinn, stunned.

"It is yours, my friend," the young alien said with a grin. "If I need another, I will simply buy one. But for now, I have no need of a starship."

And with that, he and Diyanna walked off together, multiple arms wrapped around each other as only six-armed aliens could do.

Vinset turned to the speeder, his eyes wide and his mouth open.

"This is amazing! My own ship … again."

Adam placed a hand on Vinset's shoulder. "This time, don't lose it in a card game."

Vinset looked into Adam's eyes, anxious and excited.

"So, this changes things, does it not? I mean with Starfire? I now have my own ship! Soon, we could be working for the same company, the *Human*—and the *Saznorin*—for hire."

"Is that what your race is called; I never knew."

Then Adam took Vinset by the arm and led him off the ship, and as they crossed the vast expanse of the dimly lit cavern through puddles of reflective condensation, Adam was heard saying …

"Vinset, this could be the beginning of a beautiful friendship."

The End

NEXT UP IN THE HUMAN FOR HIRE SERIES

Human for Hire (5)

Armies of the Sun

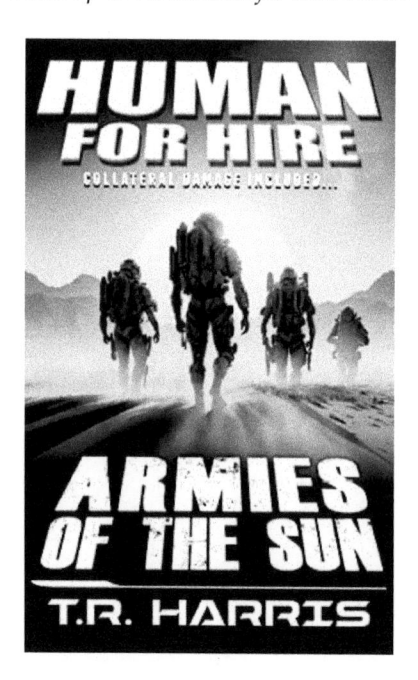

Next up in the Human for Hire Series

MORE ABOUT...

Human for Hire (5) – Armies of the Sun

THE HUMAN FOR HIRE ...

Has a particular set of skills ...

And now he's about to put them to deadly use.

Arieel Bol is the religious leader of the planet Formil, Speaker of the Gods and Carrier of the Sacred Bloodline. She also happens to be **The Human's** ex-lover and the mother of his daughter, Lila.

So when Arieel is kidnapped by a radical religious sect known as the **Armies of the Sun**, **Adam Cain** is set loose on a mad race to save Arieel before her scheduled public execution.

The Armies of the Sun have already assassinated a dozen galactic religious leaders in the past few months, and no one has been able to stop them ... until now. You see, Adam Cain (*The Human*) has a particular set of skills that makes him a nightmare for people like the Armies. He will look for the kidnappers, he will find them ... and he will kill them.

Yes, this is **Taken ... in Outer Space**. But with a twist. There's always a twist...

And the clock is ticking!

Get your copy today.

FACEBOOK GROUP

I'm inviting you to join my exclusive, secret, Super Fan Facebook Group appropriately called

Fans of T.R. Harris and The Human Chronicles Saga

Just click on the link below, and you—yes, **YOU**—may become a character in one of my books. You may not last long, and you may end up being the villain, but at least you can point to your name in one of my books – and live forever! Maybe. If I decide to use your name. It's at my discretion.

trharrisfb.com

Contact the Author

Facebook
trharrisfb.com

Email
bytrharris@hotmail.com

NOVELS BY T.R. HARRIS

Technothrillers

The Methuselah Paradox
BuzzKill

Human for Hire Series

Human For Hire
Human for Hire 2 – Soldier of Fortune
Human for Hire (3) – Devil's Gate
Human for Hire (4) – Frontier Justice
Human for Hire (5) – Armies of the Sun
Human for Hire (6) – Sirius Cargo
Human for Hire (7) – Cellblock Orion
Human for Hire (8) – Starship Andromeda
Human for Hire (9) -- Operation Antares

Human for Hire (10) – Stellar Whirlwind
Human for Hire (11) -- I Am Entropy
Human for Hire (12) – Earth Blood
Human for Hire (13) – Capella Prime

The Human Chronicles Legacy Series

Raiders of the Shadow
War of Attrition
Secondary Protocol
Lifeforce
Battle Formation
Allied Command
The Human Chronicles Legacy Series Box Set

The Adam Cain Saga

The Dead Worlds
Empires
Battle Plan
Galactic Vortex
Dark Energy
Universal Law
The Formation Code
The Quantum Enigma
Children of the Aris
The Adam Cain Saga Box Set

The Human Chronicles Saga

Novels by T.R. Harris

The Fringe Worlds
Alien Assassin
The War of Pawns
The Tactics of Revenge
The Legend of Earth
Cain's Crusaders
The Apex Predator
A Galaxy to Conquer
The Masters of War
Prelude to War
The Unreachable Stars
When Earth Reigned Supreme
A Clash of Aliens
Battlelines
The Copernicus Deception
Scorched Earth
Alien Games
The Cain Legacy
The Andromeda Mission
Last Species Standing
Invasion Force
Force of Gravity
Mission Critical
The Lost Universe
The Immortal War
Destroyer of Worlds
Phantoms

Terminus Rising
The Last Aris
The Human Chronicles Box Set Series
Box Set #1 – Books 1-5 in the series
Box Set #2 – Books 6-10 in the series
Box Set #3 – Books 11-15 in the series
Box Set #4 – Books 16-20 in the series
Box Set #5—Books 21-25 in the series
Box Set #6—Books 26-29 in the series
REV Warriors Series
REV
REV: Renegades
REV: Rebirth
REV: Revolution
REV: Retribution
REV: Revelations
REV: Resolve
REV: Requiem
REV: Rebellion
REV: Resurrection

REV Warriors Box Set – The Complete Series – 10 Books
Jason King – Agent to the Stars Series
The Unity Stone Affair
The Mystery of the Galactic Lights
Jason King: Agent to the Stars Box Set
The Drone Wars Series

BuzzKill
In collaboration with Co-Author George Wier…
The Liberation Series
Captains Malicious

Milton Keynes UK
Ingram Content Group UK Ltd.
UKHW021420011224
451693UK00012B/969